D1112290

MY WAR WITH GOGGLE-EYES

My War with Goggle-eyes

✖✖✖✖✖✖✖✖✖✖

ANNE FINE

✖✖✖✖✖✖✖✖✖✖

Little, Brown and Company

Boston · Toronto · London

The characters and events in this book
are fictitious. Any similarities to real
persons, living or dead, are coincidental
and not intended by the author.

Library of Congress Cataloging-in-Publication Data

Fine, Anne.
  Goggle-eyes/Anne Fine. — 1st U.S. ed.
  p. cm.
  Summary: Kitty is not pleased with her mother's boyfriend,
especially his views on the anti-nuclear issue, until unexpected
events prompt her, after all, to help him find his place in the
family.
  ISBN 0-316-28314-2
  [1. Single-parent family — Fiction.] I. Title.
PZ7.F495673Go 1989
[Fic] — dc 19   88-31420
                                                    CIP
                                                     AC

          10 9 8 7 6 5 4 3 2

                        HC

          Joy Street Books are published by
          Little, Brown and Company (Inc.)

      Printed in the United States of America

For my Ione

MY WAR WITH
GOGGLE-EYES

1

HELEN came into school today in the worst mood. She looked strange, and her eyes were red and puffy. She wouldn't speak to anyone, and if someone said anything to her, she simply shrugged and turned away. She buried her head in her arms on her desk lid, and waited for the first bell.

"Is anything wrong?"

A muffled, "No!"

"What's up, Helen?"

"*Nothing!*"

She lifted her head and practically spat it out. We were a little shocked. She has to be the gentlest person in our class, normally. There must have been something terribly wrong.

And you could tell that Mrs. Lupey thought so, too, when she came in.

"What's up, Helen? Anything the matter?"

Another muffled, "No!"

She didn't even raise her head, or try to sound the slightest bit polite.

Mrs. Lupey looked around at all the rest of us. With Helen's head safely buried on her desk, she let a look of: "Does anyone here have any idea what's wrong with her?" spread over her face, and we all shook our heads and shrugged.

Then the first bell rang.

"Seats, please," said Mrs. Lupey. "Roll call."

There was a note tucked in the attendance list, sent down from the office. We waited while she pulled it out of the envelope, read it, and made a little face, glancing at Helen. Then she picked up her pen.

"Number off!"

"One," called out Anna Artree. *"Two,"* shouted Leila Assim. That's how we do our roll call. It's one of Mrs. Lupey's Great Ideas to Save Time. Everyone's numbered in alphabetical order, and then each day we rattle through the numbers from one to thirty-four. I'm twenty-two.

"Eighteen." "Nineteen." "Twenty."

Silence.

(Helen is twenty-one.)

Usually Mrs. Lupey doesn't fuss. If we get held up on a number because someone's rushing through last night's homework, or scrabbling on the floor for something they've dropped, she just glances up to check they're there, and then she says the number herself, and we just carry on. This time she didn't.

"Twenty-one?"

Everyone looked toward Helen, who was still trying to bury herself in her desk lid.

"Mission Control calling Twenty-one," said Mrs. Lupey. She was watching Helen closely. "I know you're out there, Twenty-one. Speak to me. Please."

Silence. We were all watching now. When Helen Johnston acts as difficult as this, then something's very wrong.

Mrs. Lupey gave her a moment, then:

"Please . . . ? Pretty, pretty please . . . ?"

"Oh, shut *up!*" To everyone's amazement, Helen leaped to her feet and scraped her chair legs back across the floor. She lifted her desk lid and slammed it down so hard her pens flew off in all directions. "Leave me *alone,* for heaven's sake!"

And rushing across the room, she wrenched the classroom door open and banged out, leaving it swinging on its hinges.

Everyone stared.

"Well!" Mrs. Lupey said ruefully, after a moment. "I handled that really well, didn't I?"

She looked quite shaken.

"It's not *your* fault," Alice assured her. "She wouldn't speak to any of us, either. Not a word."

Mrs. Lupey glanced at the note lying on the pages of the attendance list. Then she looked thoughtfully through the open doorway. Far off, more doors were banging, one by one.

"I think I'd better send someone after her," she said. "Just to sit with her till she's calmed down."

She looked directly at me.

"Kitty," she said.

She took me totally by surprise. "Why *me?*" I squawked, and pointed across the room. "You ought to send Liz. Liz is her best friend."

"You," Mrs. Lupey said. "You are the Chosen One. Go, now, before she rushes out of school and gets run over."

Liz tried to back me up. You could tell she, too, thought Mrs. Lupey had picked the wrong person.

"Can't I go too?"

"No." Mrs. Lupey put her fingertips together and looked over them, first at me, then at Liz.

"No offense, Liz," she said. "But I think, this once, Kitty here might be just the right man for the job."

(You can see why we've ended up calling her Loopy.)

I stood and started packing my books into my schoolbag.

"Don't worry about that," said Mrs. Lupey. "Just get after her."

"But what about my classes?"

Mrs. Lupey stepped out from behind her desk and held the classroom door open.

"Go!" she said.

Extraordinary. I shoved my schoolbag under my desk, and hurried to the door.

As I went past her, she saluted me.

"We're *counting* on you, Twenty-two," she said. I think it was some sort of joke.

✄ IT WASN'T hard to work out which way she'd gone. To bang that many doors one after another, you have to be running downstairs to the coatroom. I pushed the last one open quietly.

"Helen? Are you hiding?"

There was no answer. I'm not sure that I was expecting one, but I was pretty sure she was in there somewhere. The trouble is that the coatroom is enormous — rack after rack, bulging with thick winter coats and woolen scarves. You could spend hours searching the place for missing persons.

I'm not an idiot. I used the method my sister Jude perfected to catch her gerbils each time they make one of their spectacular cage breaks. First I stepped in the room and called again: "Helen? Helen, are you *in* here?" Then I sighed, slightly impatiently, and did a quick shoe shuffle on the spot. Then I clicked the door shut firmly behind my back.

And then I waited.

It wasn't long before I heard them, the first little gerbilly scrabblings for a tissue, some long sniffs, and a huge noisy blow.

"*Got*cha!"

She sprang up like a scalded cat.

"Just go *away*!"

She looked awful, truly she did. If you'd seen her, you'd have thought everyone in her family had just been swept away by tidal waves. Her face was swollen and her nose was running. She screamed at me:

"Leave me *alone!*"

"I can't," I told her. "I've been *sent*. I'm to sit here and wait till you calm down. It's my job to make sure you don't get run over."

"Run over?" On top of distraught, she looked baffled for a moment. "Oh, run over."

This information seemed to weaken her a bit. She stopped glowering at me quite so fiercely. I took advantage of her slight softening of attitude to sweep a pair of hockey boots off the bench opposite, and sit down between two very nasty damp coats. She didn't seem to mind my being there any longer. She seemed to accept that it was my job to sit among all those dangling shoe bags and straying socks, and stop her from getting run over. It is a generally accepted fact in our school that all of the teachers and most of the parents are obsessed with the fear that one day someone will charge out of the main door without looking, and end up squashed to pulp under the wheels of some delivery van. It comes from the building's being smack on the main street in the middle of town.

Helen was groping in her pockets for tissues now. The tears were rolling down her cheeks. Her mouth hung open and her lips looked blubbery. I think her nose was blocked. She couldn't breathe.

I couldn't stand to watch. Jumping to my feet, I started rooting through everybody's pockets, coat after coat, until I came across one of those little cellophane packets of five tissues.

"Here. Take these."

Helen's so *good*. Even before she'd managed to pull one out to blow her nose, she'd peered up at the coathook to read the number, and asked in a really shaky voice,

"Whose are they?"

"For heaven's *sake*," I said. "They're only *tissues*."

I don't know if it was my impatience showing through, but Helen crumpled visibly and took to sniveling again. I felt like a real brute and cursed Mrs. Lupey for not having had the sense to send Liz. Liz would have known what to do. She was Helen's best friend. She would have put her arms around her shoulders and given her a comforting hug.

I slid my arm rather clumsily around her back and gave her a little tentative squeeze.

"Get *off!*" she snarled. "Don't *touch* me!"

"Fine!" I scuttled backward to my place on the bench opposite. "Fine by me! I won't come near you again. I'll just sit here quietly and count the coats!"

I sat there quietly, counting the coats. But I couldn't count anywhere in Helen's direction because by now she was looking such a mess it would have been embarrassing for both of us. So I just ended up staring around, desperately wishing I'd had the sense to bring down my schoolbag. At least that way I'd have had something to read. I hate sitting anywhere without a book. I'm one of those people who get all nervous when the cereal boxes are lifted off the breakfast table and there isn't anything to read anymore.

There wasn't all that much to stare at, either. We all wear the same clothes, after all. Four hundred girls' coats — just a sea of navy blue. This is a girls' school, if you can believe it. And my mother sent me here. She got fed up with my old school. She got fed up with having a fight every single morning about what I was going to wear and what I was going to put in my lunch box, and another fight every evening about all the tattered bits of paper I brought home.

"Has this been *marked?*" she'd ask, peering suspiciously at anything she found. "Why hasn't he said anything about your appalling spelling?" And if I hid my work, what I got was this: "What did you *do* all day? Not much, I bet. You know what your trouble is, don't you? You're being encouraged to grow up pig-ignorant."

That's not very nice, is it? I had to put up with a lot of that. Then one day I came home from school and made the very serious mistake of telling my mother I needed shampoo for my Science homework.

She stared.

"What are you doing in Science?"

"Care of the hair."

"*Care of the hair?*"

She went *mad.* You have never seen anything like it. She went *berserk.* Then she called up my dad in Inverness.

"Washing-her-hair lessons!" she screeched into the phone. (I had to hold the extension away from my ear.)

"Don't be so silly, Rosie," said my father. "She must be doing hair shafts, and follicles, and sebaceous glands and things like that."

Mum put her hand over the phone and bellowed at me:

"Are you doing hair shafts, and follicles, and sebaceous glands and things like that?"

I put my hand over the extension and bellowed back:

"No. Just greasy hair, and normal hair, and dry, permed, and damaged."

Then she went mad all over again. From the way she was yelling, she didn't even need the telephone. I should think everyone in Inverness could hear her without any trouble at all.

"The child is growing up *pig-ignorant,*" she told my dad. "She brings home nothing but tattered bits of paper, and sloppy projects, and she says 'spelling doesn't matter.' I'm going to find another school. Somewhere with real books and red ink and silence."

"But Kitty's happy where she is," said my dad. "You might unsettle her."

"Better unsettled than illiterate," Mum snapped, and went on to talk about how a good education was an investment for life. You'd think, to hear her going on about it, that I was a fine piece of real estate or something.

Then Dad gave up his side of the battle.

"Maybe you're right," he said. "Last time she came to stay with me I mentioned Amelia Earhart, and she thought I was talking about my cleaning lady."

"Well, there you are!" crowed Mum. "What can you expect? She does no history at all, unless you count that project on the Black Death that she does, year after year."

And that seemed to settle the matter for both of them. Mum went out and looked at every school she could find and picked the one with the most real books and red ink and silence.

The only trouble was, it was a girls' school.

"I can't go to a *girls'* school," I howled.

"Why not?" she said. "Call yourself a feminist? What's wrong with girls?"

So here I am. And I sort of like it now that I'm used to it. When you get bored with teachers droning on at you, it's better to have whole chapters of real books to read under the desk than tattered bits of paper. The silences aren't too crushing — you can always *whisper*. And sometimes you find something really nice and encouraging written at the bottom of your work in red ink. Mum's more contented, too, now that I get up and put on the same drab shapeless navy-blue uniform as everyone else every morning, and lunch boxes are forbidden. And I've stopped noticing that there are no boys.

"Helen, it's not a *boy*, is it?"

12

"*No!*"

I didn't think it was, somehow. Helen's *young* for her age, if you know what I mean. Sometimes I see her on Saturday mornings in Safeways, tagging along behind her mother's shopping cart. I saw her last week going past the detergents with a man with gray hair that stuck out just like my father's. The man was offering Helen something from a paper bag, while she stubbornly turned her face away. Maybe the two of them had just had a fight.

"Is it your dad? Have you been quarreling with him?"

"No, I *haven't!*"

She glared at me as if I were her deadliest enemy on earth.

"Oh, pardon *me.*"

"Listen," she shouted. "I didn't *ask* you to come down here. So leave me *alone!*"

Even a saint can only stand so much. I lost my temper.

"*You* listen," I shouted back. "I didn't *ask* to miss my favorite double art lesson to come down and sit in this smelly, dank hole and be snarled at by you! So be *polite.*"

I'd never get in the Samaritans. Now tears were pouring down her cheeks. She might have been standing under a cloudburst.

"Oh, Kitty," she said, her voice all wobbly. "I'm *sorry.*"

Just at that moment, through the wall, I heard the ring of the second bell. I couldn't let anyone see her in this state.

"Quick," I said. "Before everyone tramps through to classes. Get in the closet!"

I reached out and pulled her to her feet. Before she could pull back, she caught a glimpse of her reflection in the mirror between the racks. She looked a sight. Her face was blotchy where it wasn't scarlet. Puffiness around her eyes made them look piggy and bloodshot. Dried tears had stiffened all the hair around her face.

"Oooh!"

"Come *on*."

I rattled the knob of the lost-property closet until the door sprang open. It has one of those ball-bearing catches, so stiff some people always think it's locked. There is a light inside because it isn't really a closet at all, but the tiniest room with a steep sloping ceiling that fits under the back fire stairs. You can't stand up in there unless you're a midget. You have to sit on piles of everyone's lost property. It's comfortable enough, unless the gym teachers have just done one of their massive clear-outs and left nothing but one old tennis racket with busted strings and the odd rubber boot.

We were in luck. It was fairly full. I pushed Helen down on the softest-looking mound of stuff and stood guard at the door till I heard the burblings of the first people to get sent off to their classes. I waited through

14

a couple more door bangs, and then, as I expected, saw Liz prowling between the racks, looking both ways in search of her best friend.

"Helen's in here," I said, pointing.

"Is she better?"

"No. Worse."

Liz made a face. "Maybe she ought to be sent home."

From inside the closet came a strangled, "No-*oo!*"

"She doesn't want to be sent home," I told Liz.

Liz glanced behind her anxiously.

"I'm definitely not supposed to be down here," she told me. "Loopy insisted I was to stay away. 'This one is up to Kitty,' she kept saying. I think she's *mad*."

She looked at me as if I ought to be the first to leap up and agree that anyone who thought to send *me* on an errand of mercy rather than *her* had to be standing in line to sign up at the loony bin.

"Maybe you'd better run along," I suggested.

"Maybe."

She peered over her shoulder again, as if she feared Mrs. Lupey might materialize in the coatroom doorway any moment. Then, leaning forward, she called over my outstretched arm into the dark of the closet: "See you later, Helen."

She turned to me. "I'll tell Loopy you two are hiding in the closet," she said. "In case she worries that you've both gotten run over."

Then she hitched up her schoolbag and drifted off

toward the coatroom door. I caught the last few words that floated back.

"I just can't understand why she chose *you* . . ."

I didn't bother to reply. To be quite honest, I couldn't think of anything to say. I couldn't understand why I'd been chosen either. So far as I'm aware, the name Kitty Killin is not a byword for sensitivity in our faculty lounge — so why me? Why *me?* But Mrs. Lupey must have had her reasons. Helen and I must have *something* in common, apart from mothers who shop at the same Safeways, and fathers with sticky-out gray hair . . .

But I've *seen* Helen's father. He hasn't any hair at all. He is *completely bald.* And her parents have been divorced longer than mine!

I wrenched the closet door wide open. She was still sitting, hunched and miserable.

"*I* know!" I cried. "I know why you're so upset! I know why you're crying your eyes out! I know why you don't want to be sent home!"

She lifted two fierce red-rimmed little eyes that burned through the gloom of the closet like live coals.

"Your mother's going to marry that man with gray hair!"

Her mouth fell open. I felt like Sherlock Holmes on a good day.

"And you think he's a real creep! You've thought he was a creep all along, but, being the sweet Helen that you are, you've been too gentle and polite to say so. And now she's talking about your happy future together, and it's too late to explain that you don't like him."

She twisted her fingers so tightly I thought they would snap.

"Don't *like* him?" she repeated in a cold, low voice. "I can't *stand* him."

And all the color drained out of her face.

"Helen?"

I flicked the closet light switch. Luckily for her, it was the dimmest light bulb ever seen. I slipped inside and dropped on a pile of old gym shorts and sweaters. I pulled the door closed to shut us in.

"Listen," I said, leaning toward her. "No need to tell *me* about this sort of thing. I am the World's Great Expert, Helen Johnston. The stories I could tell you!"

She looked up.

"Go on, then," she said, still ashen. "*Tell* me."

"Wait till you *hear*." I pulled a rather sharp rubber boot out from underneath me and shifted till I was more comfortable. There was no hurry. We'd be left in peace. Good old Mrs. Lupey must have known from the start that it would take me hours to get through even half of it. Not for nothing has she been sloshing her red ink all over everything I've written this year — all my poems and free essays, my play in rhyming couplets, even my supposedly anonymous contributions to the school magazine. Oh yes, she knows all about what happened to me when my mother took up with Goggle-eyes.

And I knew why she'd sent *me* down, and not Liz.

2

xxx

Mum's had boyfriends before, of course. Goggle-eyes wasn't the first. For a long time it was Simon, who was tall and dark and a bit of a wimp, and wore nice suits. I liked Simon. He was the only person in the world who could sit down and help Jude with her arithmetic homework without her ending up in floods of tears. "Now you have to go next door and borrow from Mr. and Mrs. Hundreds," he'd remind her, over and over again. "Don't forget to pay back Mrs. Tens." He never got irritable, the way Mum and I do. He never abandoned her in the middle of a sum, saying, "I'm sure you've got it now." I used to sit at the other side of the kitchen table, admiring his patience, with Floss tightly clenched between my knees so she couldn't break away under the table and spread dribble and cat hairs over Simon's nice suits. Floss is friendly and sweet but she's terribly messy, and Simon works in a very posh bank.

Then Mum dumped Simon, I'm not sure why, but I suspect he was too much of a wimp for her. She went a few months without anyone, and said she rather liked it, and wasn't going to bother with men in the future. "I'd rather stay home and watch television," she said. Whenever she really needed a partner for something, she took a woman friend from work. And sometimes she borrowed Reinhardt from next door, in return for their really long loan of our ladder.

Then, one day, she met Gerald Faulkner. Don't ask me where and why and how. All I know is, one day my mother is her normal, workaday Oh-God-I-hate-my-job-I'm-going-to-resign-what's-on-TV self, and the next she's some radiant, energetic fashion plate who doesn't even *hear* when you tell her it's the last episode of her favorite series, and she's going through last year's baby-sitter list like the Grim Reaper, winnowing out all the bright teenagers who have gone off to college.

"I can't find *anyone* for Friday night!"

"Why don't you stay home and watch 'Dynasty' with us?"

She sweeps around, all fancy skirts and high heels and different eye makeup.

"Oh, sweethearts! *You* watch it, and then you can tell me what happens."

How old does she suddenly think we are? *Three?* And who was he, this man who had made all the difference? I'd heard his voice. He called up early one

19

evening before Mum even got home from work. I was the one who picked up the phone because Jude just ignores it whenever it rings. It could go on and on for hours, and she'd never bother to pick it up. She's weird that way.

I lifted the receiver and sang out hello. There was a little silence, then a voice said,

"Hello. Is that Kitty or Judith?"

"Yes," I said. (Well, it *was*.)

There was another, infinitesimal, pause. I got the feeling that, if he'd ever been introduced to me in person, he might have come out with something either funny or waspish. But all he actually said was,

"This is Gerald Faulkner. Please tell your mother I managed to get tickets, and the film starts at eight."

"Oh," I said. I hadn't realized she'd be going out again. I thought she was going to stay in and help with Jude's cardboard Roman amphitheater. There weren't any ravenous beasts yet, to put in with the gladiator.

"Thank you," he said, and then, after a pause, "Good-bye."

I didn't say anything back, so after a couple more seconds of silence, he just hung up.

I went into the kitchen, where Jude was sitting with Floss in her arms.

"That was him," I told her. "They're going out again tonight. He called you Judith."

She made a face but didn't say anything; and two

minutes later Mum came through the door, loaded with groceries and all bright-eyed.

"Did anyone phone?"

She *never* comes in asking "Did anyone phone?" If I tell her Grandma's called or Simon's called or someone from the hospital office where she works wants a quick word with her, she only *groans.*

Jude gave me a look, as if to say: *See?* And I wished that I hadn't picked up the phone in the first place. But a message is a message. So:

"Mr. Faulkner called about some film," I told her. "I expect you forgot to tell him that you were staying home tonight, to help make Jude's ravenous beasts."

She got the point.

"Sweetheart!" All guilt and glossy lipstick, she swooped down on Jude. "We'll finish your amphitheater tomorrow, I promise."

"Tonight's the last possible night." I poured cold water on this plan of hers. "We already put this off twice, remember? She has to take the whole thing to school in the morning."

Mum went out just the same at half past seven. Jude didn't seem to mind. And when I'd finished looking after the baby-sitter — making her coffee, fetching her reading glasses, finding the *TV Guide* — we all settled down to watch "Dynasty" and make ravenous beasts, though Jude's all turned out larger than hairy mammoths, and Mrs. Harrison's looked like dispirited sheep.

Then I went off to bed. I'd had enough. I hate days that start off perfectly well and then go wrong. It spoils everything. Mum can have friends, and go out and have a good time. That's fine by me. Jude and I don't want to lock her up. But watching her wriggling out of the promise she made to spend the evening at home made me feel crummy inside and second best, the way I felt the night I came downstairs and saw that Dad had moved all the boxes he'd been packing much closer to the door. They didn't see me, and I didn't make a sound. I just turned around and walked straight back up those stairs. But I let the magic marker in my hand stick out and make the thickest purple line it could all the way up the brand new wallpaper he'd spent the whole of the last month putting up, I guess because he felt he should leave us something.

Nobody heard me. I know nobody heard. But it was only a minute before Mum came. She must have followed the purple line all the way to my bedroom. But when she put her arms around me, she didn't say anything about it, not one word. And it was only then I realized it must be true, he must be leaving. Getting away had finally become more important than staying.

Still, some nights, I can't get to sleep. And that night that Mum went out with Gerald Faulkner, I was on my way back from my third trip to the bathroom before I heard Mum push open the front door, just before eleven.

I leaned against the banisters and watched her clinking about in her purse.

"Three and a half hours?" she asked Mrs. Harrison, who was already struggling into her coat.

"That's right, dear," said Mrs. Harrison. "Have you had a nice evening out with your young man?"

"Young man!" Mum snorted with amusement. "Mrs. Harrison, Gerald is over *fifty*."

"Oh, well," said Mrs. Harrison, holding Mum's shoulder to steady herself as she stepped into her rubber boots. "You know what they say. Better an old man's darling than a young man's slave!"

Mum was still giggling when she shut the door. I thought about slipping downstairs and surprising her. She could tell me about the film while we turned off the lights and unplugged the television and put the milk bottles out on the step. But something about the smile on her face put me off, and I went quietly back to bed instead.

Over fifty! Old enough to be a grandfather. Maybe he had false teeth and sagging skin, and tufts of gray hair sticking out of his ears.

Next morning, when I came downstairs, I asked her,

"When are we going to meet this Gerald Faulkner, anyway?"

I was convinced she'd be so embarrassed about him she'd drop the teapot on the spot, scalding poor Floss, and stare at me, wild-eyed. Instead she said,

"How about tomorrow? He's coming here anyway, to pick me up."

"I won't be here," I said promptly. "Tomorrow is Thursday, and I have a meeting."

So did she. She's our group treasurer, in fact. And she's usually even more fanatical about Thursday meetings than I am. I thought she'd at least *blush,* letting her private life come before what she always claims is our civic duty; but she just said, "Oh, is it Thursday tomorrow?" and flipped the toast under the grill.

She *must* have known how I was feeling. She is my mother.

"Well?" I asked. "Will you be coming to the meeting with me, or going out with him?"

She didn't take it like the challenge I meant it to be. She thought about it for a moment, and then she said:

"Oh, I think it might be a little late to tell him I'm backing out of our arrangement." And then she added brightly, as if I'd be pleased and relieved to hear it: "But you'll still have time to meet him before you go off."

"That'll be nice."

Maybe I didn't sound too keen. Why should I? If it turned out I hated him, it was too late. If *I* went out, she'd certainly make sure she got the chance to shake the boy's hand, or faint with shock, or slide the bolt firmly across the door to stop me leaving before my very first date. What could I do if I don't even get introduced until everything's rolling along very nicely?

24

Not very much.

Mum poured tea into my cup. "How did you get along with the amphitheater?" she asked, trying to change the subject.

"Just fine," I told her, between gritted teeth. "Too bad the gladiator is such a wreck. His face has shriveled and his legs are wobbly, and that carpet fluff we stuck on for his hair keeps falling out. I tell you, he looks over *fifty*."

The toast was blackening under the grill, but she eyed me very steadily indeed.

"I hope you're going to be *polite* on Thursday," she said.

✄ I KNOW a storm warning when I hear one. On Thursday I was determined to make sure that there'd be nothing in the bad-manners line that she could pin on me. When he rang the doorbell I made as if I simply hadn't heard, so it was Jude who reached the door to let him in, while I stood in the shadow at the bottom of the stairs.

He stepped inside. He was Mum's height, a little tubby, and he had silvery hair. His suit was nowhere near as stylish as any of Simon's. But then again, he wasn't a posh banker, though he did have the most enormous box of chocolates tucked under one arm.

He shifted the chocolates, and shook hands.

"Judith," he said. "Right?"

She nodded. I sidled out of the shadow.

"And Kitty."

He smiled, and kept his hand stuck out for a moment, but I pretended that I hadn't noticed it. And after one of those infinitesimal little pauses of his, he handed the huge box of chocolates to Jude.

They were those rich, dark, expensive, chocolate-coated cream mints. I've had a passion for them all my life. The box was three layers deep at the very least. I saw Jude's eyes widen to saucers.

"Are these for Mum?" she asked.

"No. They're for you."

He could have meant either *you,* or *you two.* It wasn't clear. As he spoke, he was looking at Jude, but he did glance at me briefly. It was terribly clever. It meant that when I didn't thank him along with Jude, he wasn't the least embarrassed. He didn't have to be. He might not have meant to include me at all.

"I'll tell Mum."

Jude rushed upstairs, clutching the chocolates to her chest, and Gerald Faulkner and I were left alone in the hall. I thought I'd discomfit him with my silence, but no, not at all. He simply swiveled away as though he wanted to inspect the pictures on the wall, and peered closely at a photo of me as a toddler.

"What a face!" he said admiringly. (I wasn't quite sure what he meant by that.) "It looks as if it might be you."

Really cunning, right? He doesn't actually *ask* if it's me, and then he can't look silly if I don't answer.

Just then Floss padded in through the front door,and started rubbing up against his trouser legs as if she'd known and loved him all her life. He stooped to pet her. "Puss, puss, puss." I thought now he'd be bound to try to get me to speak. It's hard to fondle someone else's cat in front of them, and not ask its name. But Gerald Faulkner's made of sterner stuff than that.

"Up you come, Buster," he said, scooping Floss up in his arms. "Who's a *nice* kitty?"

I wasn't sure what he meant by that, either. I was still trying to work it out and Floss was still purring shamelessly when Jude came thundering downstairs.

"Mum says to help yourself to a drink, and she'll be down in a minute."

"Fine."

He tipped the enraptured Floss into Jude's arms, and ambled past me with a nod, making straight for the kitchen. There was no doubt about it. He knew where he was going. I realized with a shock that Gerald Faulkner must have been in our house at least once before, maybe when Jude and I were out, or even upstairs in bed. That really rattled me, but Jude didn't even seem to notice. Or, if she did, she didn't mind. She just padded after him like a pet dog, and I was forced to lean back against the door frame so I didn't look ridiculous, standing there doggedly staring the other way.

He stood at one end of the cabinets and opened the

first two doors, looked in, then closed them. He moved along and did the same again, and again. I said nothing, just leaned against the door frame and watched. But Jude caught on before he'd gone very much further.

"Do you want glasses? They're in here."

And she rushed about, finding him the only sharp knife, and a lemon, and groping about on the floor for a couple of ice cubes that slithered off the table. The two of them kept up a steady chat about nothing at all — how quickly bottled drinks lose their fizz, how long it takes for water to freeze in an ice tray. I was astonished. Jude's not a talker, on the whole. It's like that business of the telephone. She can go hours without bothering. But here she was, burbling away merrily to this perfect stranger.

He only spoke to me directly once. He'd just pushed my schoolbag farther along the table to keep it safe from a small puddle of melted ice. The bag was open and my books were showing — not just *France Aujourd'hui* and *Modern Mathematics,* but also the things I was reading on the bus and at bedtime: *A Thousand Worst Jokes* and that thriller *Coma,* about a hospital where the anesthesia goes haywire.

He tapped the jacket of *Coma* with his knuckle.

"Is this a book about punctuation?" he asked me. "Because, if it is, the author can't spell."

I couldn't resist.

"Too bad the other book isn't *A Thousand and One Worst Jokes,*" I snapped. "You could have offered them yours."

There. I had spoken to him. I had done my bit. So I turned on my heel and walked out of the kitchen.

Mum was halfway down the stairs, wearing a frilly blouse and smart velvet pants. I glowered at her.

"Listen," she said, "I'm really *sorry* about missing the meeting tonight."

"Missing the meeting?"

That was him. He had already sneaked up behind us with the tray. I obviously wasn't going to get the chance to have a private conversation with my own mother. He was so close that I could hear the tinkling of ice and fizzing in the glasses, and smell the tang of lemons.

Mum took the glass he offered her, and smiled at him.

"Kitty and I always go together on Thursdays," she explained. "She's a bit miffed because, now that I'm not coming, she'll have to take the bus."

I *hate* it when people just assume they know the reasons for everything. I don't mind taking the bus. I never have. I like Mum to come because our car ride together to the meeting is about the only time — the only time — I'm sure I've got her on her own. That's one of the worst things about Dad moving away to Inverness. Jude and I hardly ever get to be alone with him or with Mum. We're either both with the one or we're both with the other. And they can't split themselves in two, so one of us can have a private chat down the back garden while the other is pouring out her heart on the sofa.

I was about to say "I am *not miffed*," when Gerald Faulkner touched my elbow with his, proffering his tray.

"Here," he said, nodding at the closest glass. "That one's yours."

Without thinking, I lifted the drink off the tray. I could have kicked myself. In spite of all the effort he'd put into making them, I had intended to refuse mine. But at least I could still refuse to say thank you. Unfortunately, just as Mum opened her mouth to prompt me, he waved his hand as if to cut off all the profuse and gracious thanks on which he was sure I was going to embark any second, and said, as if I were *eighteen*, or something:

"I didn't put any alcohol in yours because I didn't know if you liked the taste."

That threw Mum. She doesn't like anyone even to suggest within ten miles of my hearing that, some-day, I might be old enough to go to a bar without being sent home to bed by the bartender. For some-one to imply, even if only out of tact and politeness, that I might be on the verge of growing out of soft drinks, well, that was more than she could handle. Changing the subject as fast as she could, she plucked at the frilly blouse and the velvet pants, and asked us both:

"Are these all right?"

"Yes," I said. "They're all right." (I was still mad.)

She turned to him.

"Gerald?"

He put his head on one side. "They're lovely," he said. "Absolutely smashing. You look tremendous. But won't you spoil me a little? Wear the blue suit with those tiny pearl buttons, the black diamond stockings, and the shiny bow shoes."

I stared. I absolutely *stared*. Was he some *wardrobe* pervert, or something? Dad lived with her for years, and he could no more have described any of her clothes like that than flown up in the air. In fact, I don't think Dad even noticed what Mum wore. Obviously if she came down the stairs all dressed up to go out somewhere special, he'd say, "Oh, you look very nice." But ask her to go back up and change into something he liked even better? You have to be *joking*.

And I couldn't believe her, either. She just blushed and shrugged, and turned around to trot obediently back upstairs to change, holding her glass high. Was this my mother?

"Lucky for you this is request night," she chirruped down from the landing.

No. This was not my mother. I was still staring after the apparition in horror, when Gerald Faulkner slid one arm around Jude and one around me and steered us both into the living room.

I shook him off. He moved away and sat on the sofa. Jude made one of her nests in the beanbag. I stood and scowled.

"So," he said. "You're all mixed up in it as well."

Though I had no idea what he was talking about, I got the feeling he was speaking to me.

"Mixed up in what?"

"You know," he said, grinning. "The Tattered Banner Brigade. Close Down the Nuclear Power Plants. Ban the Bomb."

Fine, I thought. Lovely. Terrific for me. My mother's busy upstairs turning herself into some simpering Barbie doll for the sort of man she'd usually take a ten-mile hike to avoid, and I'm stuck downstairs with the political Neanderthal.

"I'm in the antinuclear movement, yes."

Tones of voice don't come much more frosty than mine was, I can tell you. It was perfectly clear I didn't want to say more. I go out and stand up for what I believe in. I have to. If I didn't, no one would know what I think. But it's a personal matter too, and my feelings are private. I didn't want to tell this grinning idiot all that it means to me. I'm caring the best way I can for everything precious: the people I love, and Floss, and my books — even the beautiful hills where Dad takes us walking each summer. I wouldn't want to talk to someone I hardly know about all that. But Gerald Faulkner didn't even notice my unwillingness to go into the matter. He was just keen on telling me what *he* thought.

"Nuclear power's been invented now," he said. "And we have nuclear bombs. You can't just pretend that we haven't. You can't *disinvent* them."

"You can't disinvent thumbscrews either," I snapped. "Or gas chambers. But you can dismantle them. And you *should*."

He spread his hands.

"But why? Nuclear weapons are our best defense."

"They're no defense at all," I said. "Bombs that poison the planet you live on can't defend you. You can't *use* them. It would just be *suicide*."

Now he was leaning forward and beaming at me. You could tell he was really getting into the discussion.

"But you won't ever *have* to use them," he argued. "Just having them around has kept the peace in Europe for forty years."

There's no point in trying to win someone over once they've made up their mind to think something different. All that happens is that you get frustrated and annoyed, and they get to practice their cruddy old arguments. *And* it's a pathetic waste of time. I've spent *hours* arguing with stubborn old geezers in the street, while dozens of potential sympathizers strolled past and never even got to see the collection can I might have been rattling under their noses. But I get so exasperated I can't keep my mouth shut.

"Some people have smoked high-tar cigarettes for forty years too, and not gotten lung cancer," I said. "But they might get it next week. Or the week after. Something's bound to go wrong some day, isn't it? What sort of peace do you call that?"

"Good enough for someone like me," he said

shortly. And he turned to Jude, safely sunk in her beanbag stuffing chocolate mints, as if to say: This conversation is over.

I should have left it there, but I was annoyed. I hate it when people insist on wrangling with you about something, then try to stop as soon as they see the arguments are no longer going all their way.

"Good enough for someone like you?" I repeated. "Maybe you mean someone as *old* as you? But it's a bit selfish not to be bothered about what might happen to the planet just because *you* won't be on it much longer."

Two spots of pink were rising on his cheeks. I could tell I was really getting to him now.

"You probably forget," he said coldly. "Someone as old as me remembers another time. A time when bombs weren't so terrible as they are now, so countries didn't have to be so careful not to start huge international wars. A time when in almost every city in Europe, orphans were picking their way through piles of stinking, smoking rubble!"

Jude lifted her head and stared. Gerald Faulkner went scarlet. I think it suddenly occurred to him he'd gotten into pretty murky waters for what was supposed to be just a friendly first meeting. And I wasn't trying to make it worse. It was only to try to comfort my worried sister that I said what I did next.

"Don't look so upset, Jude. Mr. Faulkner probably didn't have too bad a time in World War Two.

He probably spent it safe in some air-raid shelter."

"I lost my father in it. Will that do?" he snapped.

I should have felt awful, I know I should. I should have been truly ashamed and embarrassed. But somehow I wasn't. I felt angry and cheated, as if he'd somehow conjured a rabbit out of a hat to end the argument unfairly on his side. I couldn't speak to him. I couldn't say I was sorry. I just stared down at my feet and started to trace some complicated pattern with my shoe on the carpet. And it was Jude who whispered:

"How old were you?"

"About your age," he said.

Her eyes widened, but she didn't speak. He didn't seem to have anything more to say, either. So we just waited in silence, avoiding one another's eyes, till Mum came clattering down the stairs.

She threw the door open.

"Ta-*ra!*"

I expect she assumed the silence that greeted her was caused by her dramatic entrance. She certainly didn't appear to sense anything was wrong. She stepped in, swirled round twice in front of us, then made straight for the mirror, muttering:

"I think I've done up all these little pearl buttons wrong."

She looked terrific, honestly she did. I never would have thought that if she put together all the things he'd suggested, she'd end up looking as good as she did. And she was clearly pretty impressed as well.

"You're a genius, Gerald," she told him, leaning forward to see where she'd gone wrong fastening the buttons. "You ought to close down that printing business of yours, and take up dress designing instead."

"You're looking lovely, Rosalind," he told her.

Rosalind! *Nobody* calls her Rosalind. I haven't heard my mother called Rosalind since Grandma stayed here on election night and caught her swearing at some man on the television. Rosalind! I hate it when perfect strangers stroll in, quite uninvited, and don't even bother to find out what other people call themselves.

"Mum's called Rosie," I told Gerald Faulkner. "And Judith is Jude."

It was the first time I'd spoken since our argument about bombs. I said it pleasantly enough, since Mum was in the room to hear. And wouldn't you think he would at least be grateful for the information? Not him.

"Oh, I can't possibly call your mother Rosie," he said. "She's already Rosalind to me." Then he leaned toward the beanbag Jude was nesting in, and, without even asking, used a fingertip to flip a peppermint cream out of its hole. It spun high in the air, and he caught it between two fingers like a party trick, making Jude giggle. "And I can't call your sister 'Jude' either. Judith is such a lovely name. I couldn't bring myself to shorten it."

He smiled. Mum, if she saw the reflection of his expression in the mirror, might have believed that he was just being pleasant. But I was pretty sure that I could hear a message underneath: And if *you* had any fine feelings, you couldn't either.

I turned my face away. Mum was up on her toes now, practically climbing in the mirror in her attempt to see the little buttons more clearly. Her skirt rose up, revealing a couple more inches of black diamond stockings. I looked back hastily.

And, sure enough, there he was goggling at her. When Grandma catches anyone staring, she says to them tartly: "Had your eyeful yet?" But my mother's forbidden Jude and me to say that anymore, and I'd already been warned about being polite. So I just scowled at him so hard you'd think his eyeballs would have shriveled up and dropped right out of his face.

But he just kept on goggling, while Mum stepped back, satisfied with the buttons at last, and took one more look at the rest of herself in the mirror.

Her face fell. She's like me — no good at convincing herself for more than a couple of minutes that she looks all right. She plucked at the blue suit where it clung to her hips.

"Oh, dear," she sighed. "I tell you, I'm totally fed up with my body."

"Give it to me, then."

That's what he said. I *heard* him. Mum said —

no, Mum *insisted* afterward that it was just a silly joke, it meant nothing, and I should *never* have made that dreadful fuss, or yelled *"Goggle-eyes!"* at him like that, and slammed out of the door to rush off to the meeting. She said it absolutely *ruined* their evening. She said the restaurant he'd booked cost a fortune, and everything they ate ended up tasting like *carpet.* He kept on blaming himself, and she was absolutely *miserable.* She said if I ever, *ever* behaved as badly as that again, I'd be more sorry than I could *imagine.*

I said that I was sorry anyway. I told her I hadn't really meant any of the terrible things I said, but I was just a bit upset about her going out so much that week, and not helping with Jude's amphitheater like she promised, and missing the meeting. I said I wouldn't *ever* call him Goggle-eyes again, or lose my temper, and I wasn't sure why I'd been so angry with him anyway. He was kind of nice, really, I said. I didn't mind him. In fact, when the fight was finally over, and she'd put her arms around me, and I was blowing my nose over and over and trying to stop crying, I even told her that I kind of liked him, really.

➤ "AND DID YOU?" Helen leaned forward eagerly. In the small closet the shadows swayed as footfalls on the staircase overhead rocked the dim light. "Did you kind of like him, really?"

"*Like* him?" I made a face. "You have to be *joking.* I wasn't too keen on him from the start, I admit. But after that fight — " I thought back, surprised to remember so very vividly everything I felt. "After that horrible, horrible fight with Mum, I absolutely *hated* him."

3

❊❊❊

I'LL tell you this, I'd made a big mistake complaining to Mum that she was going out too much. To please me, she started staying in. But since I'd been stupid enough to say that I didn't really mind Gerald Faulkner, she'd twiddle the telephone cord around her fingers whenever he phoned to invite her to something, and say: "Oh, I don't know, Gerald. We had a really busy day at the hospital, and I'm a little tired this evening. Why don't you simply come here?"

I hated having Goggle-eyes around. I hated the whole house whenever he was in it. I can't describe exactly what it was, but it just didn't feel like home any more if he was ambling from room to room in search of a pencil to do the crossword, or slipping out of the downstairs bathroom, leaving the tank hissing behind him, or lifting my schoolbag off the coffee table so he could lean back on the sofa and watch the news on television. I hated Mum for being happy and relaxed, and nice to him. I hated Jude simply for answering whenever he asked her a trivial little question or said something casual and friendly. And sometimes I even hated sweet furry Floss for taking advantage of the fact that Goggle-eyes wasn't the most active of men, and settling on his trouser legs to shed and purr and dribble away contentedly.

But most of all, of course, I hated him.

And he knew, too. He wasn't stupid. It can't have escaped his notice that during all the evenings he spent in our house, I never once spoke to him willingly, never began a conversation, and only answered when he spoke to me if Mum was in the room to see and hear. If she was busy on the phone or in the bathroom when he said something, I'd just pretend I hadn't heard, or I'd walk out of the room, or start to play "The Muppet Show Theme" on Jude's recorder as loudly as possible. It sounds rude and childish, but that's how I *felt*. Each evening I'd hear the telltale noise of his car engine stopping at our curb, and I'd glance out of the nearest window to see him heaving himself out of the driver's seat and reaching his thumbs in the waistband of his trousers to hitch them straight before he strolled up our path. The very sight of him used to annoy me so much I'd make some excuse to slip upstairs, and I might even stay there the whole evening, pretending to read or be doing some homework, rather than come down and be forced to be civil and friendly.

Mum saw — but didn't, if you know what I mean. Oh, she knew I wasn't exactly crazy about him. She knew I'd probably just as soon he fell under a bus, or pushed off to Papua New Guinea or Kuala Lumpur, or took up with someone else's mother instead. But I don't think she had the faintest idea how strongly I felt, how much he got on my nerves, how much I loathed him.

And I couldn't talk to her about it at all. Each time I tried, I found myself standing fishing helplessly for words, and we'd just end up with her peering into my face, a little concerned and expectant, and me saying irritably: "Nothing! It doesn't matter, honestly. *Forget* it."

Once, when she was out, I tried to talk to Dad, but he wasn't very helpful.

"What's *wrong* with him, sweetheart?"

I twisted the coils of green plastic telephone wire around my little finger, and pulled hard.

"He's *horrible*. That's what wrong with him."

"What do you *mean,* horrible?"

"He's slimy."

"Slimy?"

"Yes. He's slimy and creepy and revolting. He makes me absolutely sick. I only have to glance in his direction and I want to throw up."

There was a silence. Dad means well, but he gets

to see so little of us now that often he doesn't even know where to start. In the end he asked:

"What does Jude think of him?"

There's no point in telling actual lies. They always catch up with you in the end.

"Jude sort of likes him."

"Oh, yes?" Then: "As a matter of curiosity, what does this Gerald Faulkner look like?"

"Horrible."

"Kitty, I bet this is nonsense." You could tell he was getting more confident now. "I bet this new friend of your mother's doesn't look horrible at all. I bet he looks perfectly normal — middle-aged, getting a bit fat in the middle, going a little thin on top . . ."

He might as well have been describing himself. He'd probably turned around to admire himself in his hall mirror.

"I suppose so."

I pulled the plastic wire even tighter, to make the tip of my finger go blue.

"And I suppose he has a normal face too, hasn't he? I mean, if people saw him coming down the street, they wouldn't shriek and scuttle up the nearest alley."

"*I* would."

My finger was bright purple now.

"But what's *wrong* with him?"

You could tell from the tone of his voice that he was getting as frustrated as I was with this phone call.

"Apart from the fact that he's horrible and slimy and creepy and revolting and makes me absolutely sick?"

"Yes. Apart from all that."

"I don't *know*," I wailed desperately down the telephone wire and all the way to Inverness. "I just don't *know*."

And I didn't, either. I couldn't work out what it was about Gerald Faulkner that kept me lying awake in bed imagining all those dire accidents in which I made him the star, night after night. On Monday I'd arrange for a huge industrial smokestack to topple on his head. On Tuesday he'd succumb to a grisly and incurable disease. Some drunk driver might run him over on Wednesday. On Thursday he'd lose his footing strolling with Mum along the path beside the reservoir, slip in, and drown. I tell you, I spent so much time thinking up fatal accidents for Goggle-eyes that sometimes when he turned up at our house on Friday with the customary box of chocolates under his arm, I'd catch myself feeling astonished he looked as fit and healthy as he did.

He'd step inside and scoop Floss up into his arms.

"Is Scotland playing Brazil tonight in your hall?" he'd ask, nodding at all the lights blazing away. "You know, Kitty, a clever antinuclear campaigner like you ought to go around this house and switch off a few lights. Take the pressure off your local reactor. Try and make it redundant."

I'd scowl. He'd smile, and stroll on past me into the living room where Jude would be waiting with the Monopoly or the Scrabble all set out on the coffee table. Sometimes he'd switch off a couple of lights on the way. He had a thing about wasting electricity, you could tell. Sometimes I'd catch him in the hall on his way back from the bathroom, peering at our meter, watching the little wheel spin around and around.

"You *must* have left something running," he'd tell me anxiously. "Perhaps your washing machine is stuck on spin. I can't *believe* it's going around this fast just for the lights!"

Jude would come out and giggle at him until he gave up his fretting and turned around to lead her back to their game. I'd stamp upstairs to my bedroom, flicking down every single light switch I passed on the way. And down is *on* in our house — that's how much he annoyed me.

And I annoyed him, I know I did. I was a little turd, to tell the truth. I made a point of never passing on his phone messages. I pulled snide little faces whenever he spoke. I acted as if everything he brought into our house was either potentially explosive or deadly poisonous. I wouldn't go near the fabulous shell collection he brought to show Jude when she finished with Ancient Rome and moved on to The Sea Shore, and I wouldn't be caught dead eating any of his chocolates. Oh, yes. I don't deny it. I got on his nerves as much as he got on mine.

And I was just as bad if we went out. I'd drag behind, desperately hoping that no one I knew would walk past and see him arm in arm with my mother, and think for a moment that he might be my dad. If we went to a restaurant, I wouldn't speak to him. The waiter would stand with his little pad in hand, and ask Goggle-eyes:

"Have you decided, sir?"

Goggle-eyes would lean across the table, and ask me:

"Have you decided?"

I'd turn to Mum and tell her what I wanted. She'd turn and tell him. He'd turn and tell the waiter, who'd look as politely interested as he could, given he'd already written it down on his pad. It was ridiculous, but it was important to me. And I wouldn't even taste anything Goggle-eyes ordered, or change plates with him if my meal turned out to be horrible and he was the only one willing to swap. Mum noticed. One time, when she was paying, she even leaned over suddenly and whispered sweetly in my ear:

"I'm warning you, Kits. Leave that bowl of tagliatelli in black-olive sauce just because you're too stubborn to swap it for Gerald's crispy chicken, and I'll take exactly what it cost out of your allowance."

She would, too. I know Mum. So I was forced to chomp my way down to the bottom of the vile lumpy sludge in my bowl, while he sat smirking at me over each golden delicious mouthful. I was so annoyed that

46

when the dessert cart came by, I peeled the label off one of those exotic ugli fruits and stuck it on the back of his jacket, so everyone in the restaurant would see it and snigger. And when we got home I slid his newspaper out of sight under the rug, and dropped dead leaves off the houseplants into his beer out of spite.

He tried really hard to be patient, you could tell. He spent an awful lot of time pretending he wasn't even noticing how rude I was to him. He only let his anger show once, and that was when I left one of my essays for Mrs. Lupey lying on the arm of the sofa, where he would see it the moment he sat down. I'd got a really good mark for this essay. "I hope that some parts of this, at least, spring from your very vivid imagination!" she'd written at the end. It was the essay we had to write on "Something I Hate," and I had really gone to town. *"Something I hate comes around to our house regularly,"* I wrote. *"Flabby and complacent, it acts as if it owns the place. When it breathes, all the little hairs that stick out of its nostrils waggle. Its teeth are going yellow from encroaching old age, but under its thinning hair, its scalp is mushy pink, like boiled baby. It has a really creepy way of looking at people, like a dog drooling hopefully over its food bowl. That's why I think of it as 'Goggle-eyes.'"*

I don't think he can have read any further, because it was only a matter of seconds before he ripped the paper from top to bottom and flung the pieces in the wastebasket.

I didn't mind. I'd made my point. But the look in his eyes warned me not to go so far so openly again. Oh, I kept handing in my little masterpieces at school: my "Ode to An Unwelcome Guest," my notes for a class talk entitled "Divorce Should Be Forbidden Until the Last Child Has Left Home," my descriptive essay called "An Old Man Ageing." But, for home, I kept to another, safer way of bugging him, something that I could do quite innocently in front of Mum, and no one could even tell me off.

Chattering away about Simon.

It's interesting, once you've decided to bring someone's name into the conversation, how easily it can be done. And I became an expert quite fast. In fact, I got so good at it that, after a while, there was barely a topic in the world that I couldn't, somehow, bring around to Simon. Imagine. It's evening, and Jude has finally packed up the pieces of the game that Goggle-eyes has patiently been playing with her, and gone to bed. While Mum was upstairs tucking her in for the night, he's gone through to the kitchen and made some coffee, and now she's down again, he's trying to persuade her to leave the debris of the day lying all over the carpet, and sit down beside him on the sofa to drink it. Of course, Mum has to lean over in his direction to pick her cup off the little table. And, goggling away as usual, he starts to lay it on with a trowel.

"That blouse completely changes the color of your eyes, Rosalind. They've gone the most extraordinary violet."

Op, plop. Pass the mop. I'd pluck at Mum's skirt to make it perfectly clear that I was talking to her, and not him.

"Do you remember that violet shirt of Simon's? He often wore it when he came here. Do you remember when he took us to the circus? He wore it then. And when we went to the stock-car race, and the art gallery, and the flower show. And when we visited Grandma last time."

Goggle-eyes leaned back on the sofa, raised his eyes to heaven, and let out a barely perceptible sigh. Mum said:

"Have you got any more homework to finish, Kitty?"

"No," I said. "I've done it already. I did it after I helped Jude with hers. She's stuck on fractions now. Do you remember when Simon used to help her with her homework, and you said he had the patience of a *saint?*"

Mum gave me one of her looks. To be quite fair to her, she's not at all the soppy sort of woman who goes around trying to pretend that she lived in a shoe box until the man at her side happened along. But still I could tell that she was getting really fed up with me going on and on and on about Simon, blowing it all up and stretching it out until it practically began to sound as if the two of them had broken it off about two feet away from the altar.

"And have you finished your music practice?"

"You *heard* me. I played Minuet in D and 'Gladly

My Cross I'd Bear.' Simon says when he was very young in church, he always thought that they were singing 'Gladly, my Cross-eyed Bear.' "

Simon says, Simon says . . . Behind Mum, Gerald Faulkner narrowed his eyes at me, and drew two fingers slowly and steadily across his throat. From the look on his face I could tell it was more of a joke than a real threat. But I pretended otherwise and stood up at once.

"All right. I'll go," I told them in a quiet, shaky little voice. "I see I'm in your way. I'll leave you together. I'll go upstairs and think of something to do . . ."

I let my voice trail off, trying to create the impression that I'd be sitting miserably twiddling my thumbs in a cold, lonely room until bedtime, and you could practically hear the guilt in Mum's voice when she said, "Don't be silly," and patted the sofa beside her.

"Come on. Sit down. We want you to stay. Don't we, Gerald?"

"Oh, yes," said Goggle-eyes evenly, looking at me with an entirely expressionless face. "We want you to stay. It's your home, after all, not mine."

You wouldn't think so. After a few weeks of polite sofa sitting, he practically dug himself in. He started to act as if he were one of the family. You know the sort of thing I mean. There's all the difference in the world between a guest and someone who has a right to be in your house. Guests stay where you've put them and keep on doing whatever you suggested they do, until you suggest they stop and do something else. If you leave them drinking a cup of tea and looking through your holiday slides, they're supposed to sit tight till you ask them to come and string beans in your kitchen. They're not supposed to get up the moment they feel like it and wander all over your house, rooting in your tool cupboard for hammers and wrenches, and nosing around people's bedrooms.

"Kitty, could I come in your room for a moment?"

I kept the door as tightly closed as I could, without cutting my head off.

"What for?"

He swung the hammer and the wrench.

"I'm searching for an air lock in the pipes. I think it's probably in there with you."

He nodded toward my door. And since he had his shirt-sleeves rolled right up and oily stains on his fingers, I had to believe him.

"I suppose so."

I pulled the door back as far as it would go.

He stood and waited.

"Well?" he repeated. "Can you open the door?"

"I have," I told him. "This is as far as it opens."

"What's wrong with it?" (Oh, you could see it in his eyes: *Goody! Another* little job to help me suck up to my lovely Rosalind.)

"Nothing is wrong with it," I snapped. "It's just that there's one or two books lying behind it on the floor."

"One or two books." He whistled. "You must have the whole National Scottish Collection behind there, to jam it that much."

I said nothing. I think he knew perfectly well what I meant by my silence. But I did pull the door back a little, till all my English Literature books splayed up on top of one another with their spines cracking.

He slotted himself in sideways and peered through the gloom.

"Why is it so dark in here?" he asked. "Why haven't you opened your blinds?"

I stepped back, tripping on wires from my computer and my electric curlers tangled all over the floor.

"I haven't had time yet."

"Time? It's practically evening. If you don't open them soon, it will be time to close them again."

I ignored him. He lifted a foot and slid it gingerly between my plastic bags full of spare pieces of fabric and some dirty old teacups. You could tell he was trying really hard not to step on the clothes that I hadn't had time to hang up yet. But there was not much actual carpet showing, and he tipped a cereal bowl with his heel. Luckily Floss had drunk most of the milk, and the cornflakes had dried up.

He flung the blinds open. Light flooded the room.

There was stunned silence, then:

"Dear gods!" he whispered softly in some awe. "Designer compost!"

He gazed about him in amazement. And it did look a bit slummy, I admit. Blackened banana skins don't look too awful dropped in a wastepaper basket, but when you see them spread on your crumpled bed-clothes, coated with cat hairs, they can be a bit off-putting. And the tops were off most of the makeup and hair stuff. And the playing cards would have looked neater in a pile. And if my dresser drawers had been pushed in, none of my underwear would have been spilling on the floor.

He stooped to pick up a mug with two inches of stone-cold coffee inside it, and a layer of thick green scum over the top.

"Interesting," he said. "Bit of a rarity, this particular mold."

"I think you mentioned an air lock in our pipes," I said coldly.

Notice that? Not *the* pipes. *Our* pipes. I always hoped that if I managed to make him sound enough like a trespasser in our house, he might go away. It never worked.

"Oh, yes."

He made a space for the coffee cup on my desk, between my furry slippers and a large can of cat food I must have brought up from downstairs one night when Floss seemed hungry. There was a metallic clink as he put down the cup. We both heard it. He brushed a couple of letters from my dad aside and picked up something lying underneath.

Scissors.

"Kitty," he said. "Are these the scissors your mother spent three days searching for last week?"

I flushed. I knew that he'd been at her side each time she pleaded with me to scour my room one more time, because her precious sharp hair-cutting scissors couldn't have been anywhere else but there. He'd heard me *insisting* I had looked under absolutely everything, thoroughly, twice, and they were most definitely not there.

He laid the scissors down beside the wrench with a sigh, and turned away. Brushing aside a telltale nest of crinkly wrappers from the last box of chocolates he'd brought to the house, he knelt down on the floor.

"Do you mind if I pull a few of these odd socks out from behind your radiator?" he asked politely. "Principles of convection, you understand."

"*I'll* get them out."

I wouldn't have seemed so keen to cooperate, but you know how it is when someone starts rooting around the more impenetrable areas of your bedroom. You never know if they're going to turn up something so embarrassing you'll *die* of shame.

As I reached in the top of the radiator, he tapped the bottom sharply. Two shriveled apple cores shot out.

He frowned.

"That pinging noise," he said. "It's making me just a wee bit suspicious."

I thought he meant my radiator must have sprung a leak. But when he'd fished behind the metal casing with a stick he found in my Stop Trident collection, he managed to bring up four house keys tangled together with string.

Dangling them from his fingers, Exhibit A, he looked at me gravely.

"Now these will set your mother's mind at rest," he remarked. "She's been wondering what on earth happened to all of the door keys."

He tapped the radiator again, a little harder. Another apple core shot out stuck to a chocolate that I didn't like much, and there was a rich-sounding gurgle as water welled freely along the pipes for the first time in days.

"There." He sat back on his heels. "I think that might well be the problem solved."

Brushing green eye glitter from the knees of his trousers, he stood and took one more slow marveling look around my room. His eyes, I noticed, came to rest on my potted plant.

"Fascinating," he said. "Look at it. No water. No fresh air. No sunlight. And still it lives."

"Is that it?" I asked coldly. "Are you finished?"

He turned and pulled the door back as far as it would go against my little heap of English books.

"Miss Kitty Killin," he said admiringly, edging as best he could through the narrow gap. "The only girl in the whole world who can make litter out of literature!"

Before I could stick out my tongue at him, he had gone.

4

×××

HELEN hugged her knees to her chest, and stared at me. The tears on her cheeks had dried to pale little stains, and her eyes were nowhere near as pink and swollen as before. In fact, she was looking a whole lot better.

"What *happened?*" she asked. "Don't *stop.* Go *on.* Tell me what *happened.*"

That's how I like my listeners — craving for more. Mrs. Lupey isn't Head of English in our school for nothing. She can't have forgotten that the tears rolled down her cheeks when she read my collection of sixteenth-century limericks entitled *Go Home, Old Man, from Whence Thou Camest.* She must remember that she chewed her nails down to the quick reading my essay "Will She, Won't She Marry Him?" She begged for the last installment of my serial *Tales from a Once Happy Home.* Oh, yes. Mrs. Lupey knew one

57

thing when she passed over Liz for Mission Helen and sent me out instead.

When it comes to a story, I just tell 'em better.

✄ I DIDN'T stay there sticking my tongue out at thin air for long. I followed him downstairs. Of course I did. I needed to know what he was going to say about finding the scissors. I thought I'd end up in a colossal fight.

I waited till he'd gone into the kitchen, and then slipped down as quietly as I could, leaning on the banister rail to take weight off the stairs that creak. When I got close enough to hear what they were saying, the kitchen door swung open a couple of inches, and I could see Mum dealing laundry into piles on the table as fast as a croupier at a casino.

"Mine. Kitty's. Jude's. These socks are mine, I think. Kitty's — no, she's grown out of it, it must be Jude's now. Mine. Kitty's. Mine."

Goggle-eyes must have been rinsing grime from the radiators off his hands. I could hear water splashing in the sink as he said:

"Why don't you get one of the girls to help you?"

Mum laughed her hollow laugh, "Oh, ho, ho, ho!" Then she threw down the last of the socks. "Jude's. Kitty's. Mine. That's it!"

Lifting the nearest pile, which happened to be mine, she made for the door. But he stepped in front of her and took the clothes from her arms. I couldn't see the expression on his face, but I've no doubt that he was goggling at her as usual, because she was blushing when she protested:

"No. Let *me* take them."

"No. Let *her*."

Wrenching the door fully open so I was forced to duck beneath the banisters, he bellowed up the stairs:

"Kitty! Come down and fetch your laundry from your mother!"

"And hang it neatly on your floor," said Mum.

Goggle-eyes turned, and told her in stern tones:

"It's not a joke, Rosalind. Kitty's room is a *pit*."

I saw Mum's grin fade pretty fast, and I knew why. Mum's like me. She hates it when people speak out of turn about things they don't understand. What Goggle-eyes didn't know was that Mum used to be at me all the time about my room, threatening and cajoling, stopping my allowance and forbidding me to go out with my friends until it was tidy. She must have spent entire *weeks* of her life fighting the battle of my room with me, going on and on about it until, once every couple of weeks or so, I used to crack and reckon it was probably less trouble to clean it up than keep on arguing that it's my room and I should be allowed to keep it how I like. But after Dad left home, Mum just gave up. We had one or two last horrible fights about the mess, and then she suddenly seemed to throw her hands up about the whole business. I think, once she was on her own, she simply couldn't face the effort and unpleasantness of all that endless nagging and scolding.

What did old Goggle-eyes know about that? Nothing. He didn't live with us. He didn't know us. He didn't understand that I'm one of those people who practically only have to *glance* in a room for it to begin to look as if a bomb hit it. If my poor Mum stayed on my case long and hard enough to keep my room picked up all the time, she'd have to give up *hours* of her time. She'd probably have to give up *work*.

Mum has her pride. She wasn't going to tell Gerald Faulkner that, now my father wasn't in the house to back her up through every battle, she'd had to make a virtue of necessity and throw in the sponge. Keeping her tone light, she just said to him:

"Oh, take it easy, Gerald. Maybe you've just forgotten what kids Kitty's age are like."

"Don't try to tell me they all have floors thick with tangled electrical wires, and filthy dishes, and books in great untidy heaps!"

Mum was still trying to make light of it.

"I call it her open-plan filing system."

"I call it *disgusting*."

He put his foot in it there. It was quite clear from the expression on Mum's face that, for the moment, she had heard enough from Gerald Faulkner about his views on natty housekeeping. Purposefully silent, she reached out for the laundry pile.

But Goggle-eyes refused to hand it over. He hadn't finished yet.

"You're doing your girls no favors," he lectured. "Letting them get away with murder."

That really rattled Mum.

"*Murder?*" she snapped. "For heaven's sake, Gerald! Look at the planet we live on! Wars. Famine. Poverty. These things bring misery to half the world! Ten million pounds a *minute* is spent on arms! My Kitty spends her time coming with me to meetings, raising money by shaking collecting cans, and trying to let the taxpayers of this country know that, for the cost of one *single* nuclear weapons system, we could afford a decent health service!" She waved her arms in a flamboyant gesture. "What does it *matter* if her bedroom floor is knee-deep in undies?"

Time to stop eavesdropping, and push the door open fast! I wasn't going to risk hearing his answer to *that* one!

"Ah!" he said, hearing me come in. "At last!"

He turned and dumped the laundry in my arms.

"There you are," he said cheerfully. "Another forkful for your compost heap."

I thought what he said was rather funny actually (though I would rather have *died* than smiled). But for some reason a look of real irritation crossed Mum's face. Her lips set in the way they did when she and Dad were on the verge of arguing.

"Gerald," she said coldly. "It's not my children's

fault I always reckoned I had better things to do with my time than stand over them while they folded their clothes and put their things away neatly. So please try not to pick on Kitty because, like me, she now thinks there are more important things in life than properly made beds and tidy sock drawers!"

I caught my breath. Dad absolutely *hates* it when Mum goes all tight-lipped and snooty on him. He scowls and snaps right back.

But Goggle-eyes was unruffled. In fact, he was standing there grinning his head off.

"Rosalind!" he said. "How can you talk such utter baloney?"

I think Mum was speechless from shock. (I know I was speechless from terror.) But Goggle-eyes was still beaming.

"What you say sounds so lofty, so high-minded! But it's pure rubbish."

"*Rubbish?*" Poor Mum was mouthing like a fish.

"Yes, *rubbish*. And I'll tell you why." He waved a hand toward the ceiling. "I happened to walk past your bathroom half an hour ago, and, being the tidy sort of fellow I am, I couldn't help noticing that it was in a shocking state. Simply shocking! Filthy rings around the tub. Teacups and clothes everywhere. Soggy comics on the floor. Why, the room was ab-solutely *festooned* with paper."

Mum opened her mouth to interrupt, but he lifted his hand to stop her, and pressed on.

"Then what happened, Rosalind? I walked by

twenty minutes later and it looked perfect. Clear floor, clean tub, nice gleaming surfaces. Who cleaned it up? Not me. I was still scouring the house for that air lock. Not Judith. She's out there swinging upside down in the park. And I'll bet that it wasn't Kitty here. I'd be prepared to put my life savings on that!"

I gave him the sour look that he deserved, but he didn't notice. He was too busy smiling at Mum.

"So who pitched in there with the wet mop, Rosalind? Who wiped the mirrors and the faucets? Who was it took time off from going to meetings, and shaking cans in the street, and calling for an end to the arms race? Who was it cleaned up the bathroom?"

Mum went bright pink.

"See!" he crowed. "It was *you*. Of *course* it was. And all I'm saying is that every now and again, a serious and committed citizen like yourself could do with a little bit of help with the housework from equally serious and committed Kitty here!"

The look I gave him would have shriveled Rasputin. Oh, it was definitely the evil eye. But I was on my own now. Mum's face, as well as his, was wreathed in smiles.

"Take care, Gerald," she giggled. "Mind what you say! You'll end up in terrible trouble with Kitty."

"Don't worry," he said. "I'm not afraid of Kitty. I'm not afraid of anyone. And I always say exactly what I think."

He didn't have to tell *me*. I'd already noticed. I'd

not forgotten that he took advantage of our very first meeting to trash all my views on nuclear arms. And I'd had plenty of opportunities since then to notice he always spoke his mind — though, to be fair, he'd wade in on anybody's side. I'd thought at first, because he was so stuck on Mum, he'd end up taking her part whenever he could, and staying tactfully quiet on the sidelines whenever he couldn't. But it turned out he wasn't like that.

And it wasn't because he couldn't keep his big mouth shut. He'd proved that he could be as quiet as the grave when he chose. I was quite sure that he had never breathed a word to Mum about that spiteful essay about him I wrote for Mrs. Lupey and left around for him to see. But, even so, my heart began to thump like mad when Mum finally moved the last of the laundry aside, and picked up the hammer and wrench he had laid on the table, revealing her precious scissors underneath.

"My scissors! You *found* them!"

I didn't take my eyes off him for a second. Though he said nothing at all, he did let his face break into one of those sunny smiles of his, and he shrugged very lightly.

Mum, of course, jumped to the simplest conclusion.

"I can't *believe* it! I must be going crazy. Imagine putting my scissors away in the toolbox!"

Still he said nothing, though he glanced at me.

"Good thing the pipes blocked," Mum went on,

sweeping the scissors up to safety on their special hook. "Otherwise these might not have shown up for *weeks*."

"That's true," he said.

He didn't wink at me — no, not exactly. But one of his eyelids did flicker a little, I saw it, though I would rather have *died* than catch his eye and let myself wink back.

I did feel grateful, though. He'd saved my skin. To show him I understood that, I dropped my pile of laundry down on Jude's, and said, scooping them both up in my arms:

"I'll do the whole business, since I'm going up there."

"Would you?" Mum looked pleased. "That's a help."

I didn't wait for praise from Goggle-eyes. I took the clothes upstairs and put them away. While I was at it, I picked up all the dirty cups and bowls and plates lying around my room — there was a stack of them — and carried them down, along with the can of stale cat food.

I found Mum rooting on the pantry floor.

"Kitty, any chance of your getting me some potatoes?"

"Can't it wait till I get back?"

She looked up.

"Where are you going?"

"To the library."

Mum frowned. She's fed up with libraries. She's been fed up with them for weeks, making life very difficult for me and Jude. She used to be dead keen. Like everyone else, she had this rosy vision of libraries as cool and silent repositories of neatly shelved wisdom: temples of learning, gems of culture, high points of civilization, that sort of thing. If I said I was going to the library, she'd smile and go all soft inside, and you could tell she was thinking, whatever her faults, she couldn't have failed too badly as a parent. At least we still used the library.

Then things began to go sour. First Jude came home one day insisting Floss needed four separate injections to keep her breathing safely through the winter. When, two weeks later, a bill came from the vet for fifteen pounds, Mum asked Jude irritably: "Where did you hear about these injections, anyway?" Jude answered innocently enough: "There was a notice on the library wall," and that was the start of Mum's steady disenchantment. I thought she might march straight in there and complain.

Then, two or three weeks later, I came home *destroyed* because I'd stood around for half an hour, unable to peel my eyes from some terrible video they were showing over and over in the foyer about the tactics of the South African police. Mum phoned the chief librarian about that. Then Jude had nightmares for a fortnight after the old antivivisection poster of white mice in a cage was taken down and replaced by one far more vivid and heartrending, featuring a cat that looked for all the world just like our Floss.

So things were set fair for trouble already. But how was I to know that only that morning Jude had made the serious mistake of telling our rather touchy neighbors they ought to be worming their dog far more often (Courtesy: Library Fact Sheet No. 44), and Mum had only just got back from trying to make peace next door.

"*Why* are you going to the library?" she asked suspiciously, through gritted teeth.

"I want to get something."

"A book?"

"Not exactly."

"What, then?"

I didn't answer on the grounds that it might incriminate me.

"A *computer* game? Right?"

Guiltily, I nodded.

"That's it!" she shrieked. "That's it! Finito! From now on that stupid library is off-limits. It's *out of bounds!*"

I raised my eyes to heaven. Goggle-eyes burst out laughing. Mum turned on him.

"All very well for you to laugh!" she told him. "I bet you never had this trouble when your boys were children!"

I stared. I hadn't realised he had grown-up sons.

Mum sighed. "You were *lucky. Your* children grew up in the good old days when libraries were libraries! I bet your boys used to stroll down there and spend a quiet half hour or so choosing real *books.* Then they'd come home, and you'd have at least a couple of hours peace while they sat down and read them, cover to cover."

Still beaming, Goggle-eyes nodded. *Yes,* his face said. *That's how it was back in the good old days.*

"Well, things are different now," Mum snapped. "They're back home in under ten minutes with some stupid pip-pip-pipping computer game stuck under their arm, and all you hear for hours after they get back is 'Shouldn't we play it safe, and join the automobile club, Mum?' And 'Can I take Swahili classes at the university extension, Mum?' and 'What *is* crack, Mum?' "

She leaned across and snapped her fingers in my face.

"Well, that's *it!*" she said again. "The party's *over.* Speaking both as a parent and a taxpayer, I have to announce that libraries are now far more trouble than they're worth. You can just go upstairs and shelve the few shabby books you have in alphabetical order."

"The library doesn't keep books in alphabetical order any longer," I told her.

Her mouth dropped open, honestly it did.

"I beg your pardon?" she said softly. "Have the

heavens fallen? Tell me, Gerald. Did I hear what my daughter said?"

"It's *true*," I said, before he could chime in. "The children's section is all done by dots now. Red dots for teenage, blue for middle school, pink for the primary, and green for preschool."

"You're joking! You are *joking! Dots?*"

"Well — little round stickers, really."

Mum buried her head in her hands.

"Little round stickers," she groaned. "Gerald, it's finally happened. The barbarians have taken over." She lifted her head. "But why are they waiting?" she suddenly demanded. "What's holding them up? Why don't they just tear down the bookshelves and hurl the books into four huge piles: *Boring, All Right, Pretty Good,* and *Brilliant!*"

Goggle-eyes' shoulders were heaving with laughter. Mum turned on him.

"No, *honestly*," she insisted. "I'm *serious*. Why pretend any longer? What does it matter that we, the British public, once had a library system that was *the envy of the world?*"

She might have been onstage in the West End. Poor Goggle-eyes was wiping tears of laughter from his cheeks. I raised my eyes to heaven yet again.

Then Mum stuck out her hand dramatically.

"Give me your library card. Go on. Hand it over."

I shook my head and jumped back fast.

"Come on," she said. "Hand it over. It's confiscated."

"Oh, no it isn't!" I said, theatrically.

"Oh, yes it is!"

"Oh, no it isn't!"

All the time, keeping the table between us, I kept moving steadily and stealthily toward the back door. Mum suddenly made as if to chase me; and, making a huge effort, Gerald Faulkner managed to control his laughter long enough to catch her in his arms and hold her back, while I got safely through the door.

"Bye-*eee!*" I called, tearing down the walk.

I sang all the way to the library. I couldn't help it. One or two people stared (I'm not the greatest singer in the world) but I didn't care. I felt light and happy. It always cheers me up when Mum stops worrying about work, or the mortgage, or how we're turning out, and just acts silly. And it seemed *ages* since we'd had a really silly scene like that, with her halfway serious and halfway fooling, and not caring for a moment how everything turned out.

And maybe it had helped, having Goggle-eyes there watching everything, laughing. Maybe Mum just felt far more cheerful when she had company. She and Dad used to play the fool quite a bit before things went wrong. Maybe there were advantages to having someone else around the place.

I thought about it a lot while I was in the library. And then again when I walked home, the long way, and saw Jude hanging upside down from the park railings, her hair sweeping the grass. She'd taken to him, too, right from the start. She'd let him help her with her project on The Sea Shore, she ate his chocolates, and she sat on his knees through all the repeats of the old Cosby shows. I'd watch her out of the corner of my eye, practically getting rolled off his lap onto the floor whenever something struck Goggle-eyes as particularly amusing. It didn't seem to bother Jude that she was curled in the arms of the opposition, a die-hard, reds-under-the-beds deterrent-monger who actually *believes* that on the day nuclear weapons are dismantled in Britain, Russians will march in from Moscow, stamping the snow from the steppes off their feet.

And it didn't seem to bother Mum either (though she at least did make the effort to point out to him that countries like Norway and Sweden and Austria are *miles* nearer Russia than we are, and don't have nuclear weapons, and aren't invaded).

Maybe I shouldn't let it bother me.

I came home prepared to give it a real try. I know I did. I came home with feelings toward Gerald Faulkner that weren't exactly *warm,* but they were neutral. He'd done me more than one good favor that day. He might not be well and truly tuned in to Small Planet Earth, but he did have his good points. How was I to know that, within *seconds* of my stepping in the house, he'd blow it? Stand there like the Grand Inquisitor, and send himself hurtling right back to the top of my hit list.

"Let me get this straight." He rested both hands

on the table and leaned across. "Kitty has just dug those potatoes out of the ground for you."

"Correct," said Mum, dumping the sodden black lumps into the sink and turning the full force of the water on them, to rinse off the soil.

"And they're from the vegetable plot at the bottom of the garden."

"The very same."

"Begun by her father, but now kept up by Kitty with a bit of help from Judith."

"Not *much* help," I reminded everyone. (Jude spends all her free time out in that park.)

Ignoring me, Prosecuting Counsel turned to Mum, his Star Witness.

"And you buy all the seeds."

"Right."

"And the gardening tools."

"Everything," said Mum. "Shovels, beanpoles, fertilizers, netting, manure . . ."

"And Kitty *charges* you for the potatoes!"

I stared.

"What's wrong with that?"

I was astonished, simply *astonished*. You'd think I was a *bag snatcher* or something, the way he was looking at me, all shocked and disapproving.

"I think it's simply appalling," he replied.

For heaven's *sake*.

"*Why?*" I argued. "I don't *like* gardening. Neither does Mum. It's a big chore. So now that Dad's gone, Mum pays me for the vegetables, to keep me going."

"What about *you?*" he demanded. "Have you paid *her* yet for the lunch she cooked, the rugs she vacuumed, and the bathroom she cleaned?"

Mum tried to stick up for me then.

"But, Gerald. I'm her *mother.*"

"You are her *family,*" Goggle-eyes corrected. "And she is yours. You shouldn't be *paying* for her cooperation. *No one* should have to bribe their close relations to pull their weight. It is *disgusting.*"

Mum made a face. I thought, at first, it was a mind-your-own-beeswax-Gerald sort of face at him. But then I realised, to my horror, it was a just-a-minute-while-I-think-about-this sort of face.

"It certainly works, though," she told him after a moment. "Look how promptly Kitty brought in the potatoes."

"That's not the point."

Mum wrinkled her nose again. You couldn't tell what she was thinking. It might have been that's-what-*you*-think; but, then again, it might have been maybe-you're-right.

It was maybe-you're-right.

"Maybe you're right. I must say, I've never felt quite right about it. I used to help my parents in the house, and they would never have dreamed of giving me money."

"I should think not. The whole idea is repellent."

The very certainty with which he pontificated made Mum pitch in again on my side.

"But, Gerald. It does seem fairer to pay Kitty *something,* now Judith's big enough to do her share, yet never does."

Goggle-eyes spread his hands.

"Rosalind," he said, as if he were talking to a small child or an idiot. "If anything, you should be fining Judith till she does fair shares, not handing out great bribes to Kitty."

"Great bribes!" I muttered. "Ten miserable pence a pound!"

He turned on me.

"Oh, ho!" he crowed. "Be warned, all mothers everywhere! Already she's angling for a raise, our little vegetable entrepreneur!"

Mum laughed.

"Oh dear, Kitty. Looks as if, if Gerald gets his way, your potato plans are blighted!"

I suppose, looking back, she only intended it as some harmless little vegetable joke. But I must say I didn't find it funny. I felt humiliated, standing there with muddy hands, while those two stood arm in arm beside the sink, grinning.

On any other day, I would have lost my temper. I would have forgotten my promise, and yelled at him to bug off with his goggle-eyes, stop sticking his nose into other people's business, clear off, go *home!*

But, that day, I'd been feeling so *happy*. All the way to the library, and all the way home, the world had suddenly seemed so huge and colorful, the wind so puffy and fresh, the skies so *high*. To come home in such tremendous spirits and pull Dad's heavy spade out of the shed to dig up spuds for Mum because I love her and she was happy today too — and then to come through the door and, within seconds, find that the carping had begun again . . .

Well, it was all too much. I burst out crying. To be quite honest, I didn't even *burst*. I just began to cry, like a baby. Tears pricked behind my eyes, and before I could stop them — before I could even spin around and rush out of the room — they'd welled up and over, spilled down my cheeks, and splashed like inkblots on my muddy shoes.

"Kitty! Oh, Kitty! Dearest!"

Pulling herself free, Mum was across the kitchen in a flash, and had her arms around me.

"Kitty, my *love*."

I'll say this much for him, he had the grace to disappear without a word. And as soon as the door shut behind him, Mum asked:

"What's *up*, Kits? Kitty-kat, *tell* me."

I scraped huge tears away with muddy palms.

"I'm just fed up with him," I told her. "He's *always* here now, practically every day. You're not the same. I know you try to be, but you're just *different* when he's around. And he keeps saying what he thinks all the time, and what he thinks is never what we think, and I'm just *sick* of him."

The tears were making me hiccup. Mum sat down on the nearest chair and pulled me on her lap. Tugging the bottom of my shirt out of my jeans, she used the flap of it to wipe the mudstains off my cheeks. I must have looked like a total idiot — I'm practically as tall as Mum — but I didn't care.

"I think I've just had *enough* of him for a while. I feel *squashed*."

Mum patted my damp knees.

"I'll tell you what," she said, just like she used to when I was little and lost something precious, or had a bad fight, or couldn't go to two birthday parties at once. "I'll tell you what. We'll make a deal. You hang on through the weekend, then I won't invite Gerald all next week. We'll phone your dad, and maybe you can go to Inverness next Friday, for a change. Then we'll have one more quiet week at home. Afterward, Gerald can come for lunch on the weekend, and maybe by then you won't be feeling so *squashed*."

"Why can't we start now?" I sniveled. "Why do I have to hang on through the weekend? Why can't we have tomorrow to ourselves?"

"But Kitty," she said. "Tomorrow is Sunday. It's the trip to the submarine base."

I'd clean forgotten about that. I shouldn't have, either. I'm one of the members of the committee that arranged it. Some other local group had booked a bus, and now they couldn't fill it. Our people had offered to pitch in and help.

But that would be all right. The three of us have always gone on these things as a family.

"Well, we'll be by ourselves."

Mum shook her head.

"No, we won't. Gerald's coming."

"Oh, no!" I couldn't help it. I just started howling all over again. "*Why* is he coming? He doesn't even believe in what we're doing."

Mum looked embarrassed, but she answered firmly enough:

"Kitty, he asked if he could come along, and I said yes."

"Tell him you've changed your mind!"

Mum looked distressed too, now.

"I can't," she said at last. "I'm sorry. I would if I could, but I *can't*. I don't mind telling him the truth — that you'd prefer it if he didn't come; but I can't tell him that I've changed *my* mind."

I sat slumped on her knees with my arms around her neck. Half of me would give anything in the world to have the three of us — Mum, Jude, and me — on our own for one day. The other half was absolutely determined that Goggle-eyes would never know he could upset me so much.

I rubbed my eyes.

"Don't *tell* him," I said fiercely. "*Promise* me. He

can come with us tomorrow. But only if you don't tell him that I *mind*."

"I promise. I won't say a *word*."

I slid off her lap before her blood supply was cut off for so long she ended up with gangrene.

"I'll go and wash my face."

I crept as silently as I could through the hall. I needn't have worried about being overheard. The living room door was only open a crack. Jude and Gerald were sitting together on the sofa. She had her arm around his neck the same way that she used to cling to Dad, and he was reading her the stock market report.

"The FT-SE share index finished a volatile session nursing a 44.9 points fall at 1,658.4 yesterday," he droned. "At one time it had been down 105.3 points."

Jude's thumb slid in her mouth, and her eyes closed.

"The FT-30 share index closed 33.5 points down at 1,288.5. Government stocks were firm . . ."

I went on upstairs. I felt terrible. Being outnumbered is horrid at the best of times. But when you know that everyone you care about will feel rotten if you get your way, getting your way goes sour. Whose feelings count for most? And why? I'll tell you one thing I'm quite sure about: things are much *simpler* when it's your real dad.

✀ "YOU'RE TELLING *me*."

Whoops! Wrapped up entirely in my own brilliant storytelling, I'd totally forgotten this was her problem too. But Helen didn't get a chance to start telling me about it because, just at that very moment, there was a sharp rat-a-tat-tat on the door.

I thought it must be Liz, nosing about again in break time. I was about to shout, "Go away!" when the quite unmistakable timbre of Mrs. Lupey's voice came effortlessly through the thick wooden panels of the door.

"Mission Control calling Lost Property Capsule. How are things going in there?"

I couldn't think what to answer, so I shouted back: "Fine!"

"Helen?"

Helen took a deep breath. I think she was testing herself with some private psychic dipstick. Then she called:

"I'm feeling much better, Mrs. Lupey."

"*What?*"

(Helen's voice just doesn't have the same wood-penetrating qualities as mine and Mrs. Lupey's.)

"She says she's feeling much *better!*" I yelled.

"But is she coming *out?*" bellowed Mrs. Lupey. "Intergalactic time passes. Whole lessons are being missed. What are the chances of a dual return to base?"

I peered at Helen, who shook her head like a small child who thinks it's being a real daredevil.

"Not yet," she whispered. "I want to hear what happened to *you* first."

"Delicate mission under way," I yelled. "Briefing

not yet fully accomplished. This capsule needs more time before it's ordered to return to base."

(I've always found that, if you play along with them, you can get anything you want.)

"All right, then, Number Twenty-two," she said. "I'll take your word for it."

And off she went.

5
✕✕✕

I CAN'T say Goggle-eyes made the world's greatest effort to fit in well on our trip to the submarine base. For one thing he turned up at the rendezvous wearing his best suit, a striped tie, and freshly polished shoes.

"You're going to get filthy!" said Mum.

"Oh, yes?" Goggle-eyes was already eyeing our grubby windbreakers and hiking boots with some disfavor. "Holding the demonstration in a pigsty, are we?"

Mum thought it better to take this as a joke.

"There's a bit of a walk over some Ministry of Defense land when we get there," she explained. "We're planning to reclaim the hills."

"Are we, indeed?" From the expression on his face it was perfectly clear that, to Gerald Faulkner, reclaiming hills meant, at the very least, cutting holes in expensive barbed wire fences, overwhelming the military police in an act of mass trespass, and rushing, shrieking and whooping, down on unguarded stockpiles of nuclear warheads. I caught Mum's eye. *Mistake! Mistake!* I flashed at her in family semaphore. *Quick. Send him home before the bus comes and it's all too late.*

Mum got the message.

"Gerald," she said gently. "Are you *sure* that you want to bother to come with us today? You wouldn't be just as happy at home with your feet up, reading the papers?"

"I'd be happier," he said, looking around meaningfully at our straggling group of early morning yawners. "*Much* happier."

"Well, then — "

"No," he insisted, shaking his head firmly and dashing all my hopes of a nice day. "I've said I'm coming with you, and I'm coming."

I couldn't help asking him the question.

"But *why?*"

He stared.

"Well, for the pleasure of your company, of course."

I was mystified.

"But you have the pleasure of our company practically every *day,*" I reminded him. "It's *crazy* to want an extra day of it."

"I don't see that," he said equably, taking my arm. "Surely wanting an extra day of your company is no crazier than wanting your company at all."

When someone's in that mood, there's no point arguing. So I didn't, even when the huge bus that had been hired finally showed up, and he climbed on and plunked himself down in the seat beside Mum without even asking Jude or me whether we minded. Jude didn't, as it happened. She was quite happy to slip in the seat behind without arguing. I didn't argue either. But I did *mind*.

I took the window seat — Jude didn't care. I could see the reflection of the side of Mum's face in the glass, and if I leaned sideways I could watch Goggle-eyes through the gap between the seats. After a while the bus driver insisted that, even if we had been expecting more people, we really ought to go or we'd never get there. The smokers ground out their last cigarettes and climbed aboard, wheezing and coughing. And I saw Goggle-eyes looking pointedly at his watch. Personally, I thought the fact that we were only twenty minutes late leaving robbed his snide little gesture of a lot of its punch; but he didn't know that we're usually later.

The bus rolled through the fields and villages, and gradually everybody stopped yawning and flicking through their Sunday newspapers and started to chat. Somehow you didn't get the feeling that Goggle-eyes was putting himself out to make friends. I overheard him telling the shy wind-power engineer sitting across the aisle: "Personally, I think windmill parks are an eyesore"; and when Beth Roberts' small son tugged at his newspaper to see the cartoon, he said quite unnecessarily loudly and clearly: "Do you mind if I finish reading it before you recycle it?" He sneered visibly through the sing-along Josie organised, not even joining in the easy choruses like "Take the Toys from the Boys," and "What Shall We Do With the Nuclear Waste?" All in all he was a total pain, and I could tell that practically everybody who took the time to be friendly when they were walking up and down the aisle finished up by assuming that he must be some police spy.

It seemed a very long ride. He spent a lot of it tormenting Mum.

"How come so few people ended up coming today, Rosalind?"

It was true that the bus was half-empty. I heard the caution in Mum's voice as she replied: "Sometimes the phone tree doesn't work too well."

"Phone tree?"

Oh, you could *hear* glee gathering in his voice. He knew that he had a winner here. And so did Mum.

"It's how we send last-minute messages," she admitted. "Each of us knows the numbers of two others, and each of them phones two more, and so on. When it works well, the phone tree branches out quickly."

"I see," said Goggle-eyes. There was one of those dangerous little pauses of his before he added provocatively: "A sort of urban bush telegraph?"

Mum turned her head away and gazed out of the window. Her reflection was so blurred that I couldn't make out her expression. Was she trying not to lose

84

her temper? Or was she trying not to laugh? I couldn't tell. But I know how I felt. I felt like reaching over the back of his seat and pulling hanks of his thin silvery hair out of his boiled-baby pink skull, and yelling at him that he could sneer all he liked at our warm windbreakers and buses that leave late, and makeshift ways of passing messages; but, unlike the Ministry of Defense, we didn't have billions of pounds a year of taxpayers' money to keep our organization running like clockwork.

What was the point, though? You never get anywhere trying to explain things to someone like Gerald Faulkner. Mum says, "Just save your breath to cool your porridge." When people sneer at what we think and what we do, she only smiles.

"Don't let them *bother* you," she used to tell me whenever I got mad. "That's the way history goes. All change takes time. Everyone who ever tried to change anything important got sneered at by those who wanted things left the same. Look at the people who fought for the end of slavery! 'Meddlers! Ignoramuses! Troublemakers!' Look at the women who fought for their right to the vote! 'Pushy hoydens! Vandals! Disgraces to their sex!' All it proves is that we're getting somewhere."

"Oh, yes," I said. "Where?"

(I was feeling really grumpy and dispirited that day, I remember.)

"Listen," she said. "The problem is when the people in power don't even *notice* you. It's only when you get strong that they start sneering and calling you foolish and misguided. That's the first step. Then more and more people come around to your way of thinking, and you get stronger and stronger. They get more worried. You can always tell. That's when they start to call you dangerous as well as foolish, and try to encourage everyone who isn't on your side yet to come out of the woodwork and sneer at you too."

"Well, it's not very pleasant!"

"No. It's not pleasant. But it has always happened that way, and it always will."

"Then what?" (I mean, nobody likes to think that they're in for a lifetime of sneering.)

"Then you win, of course," she said. "Why would they bother to make fun of your homemade banners and your muddy boots if they could polish off your arguments?" She grinned. She was terribly cheerful about it. "I'll tell you one thing I learned from studying history, Kitty. As soon as you see your opponents are reduced to insulting you, you know you're on the way to victory."

That's what my mother said. That's what she told me, and I trust her. That's why I managed to stay sitting fair and square on the seat, and not jump up and down shrieking at Goggle-eyes, and pulling the hair out of his head in handfuls. I'm well brought up, I am. I've got self-control.

Which is a lot more than you can say for him. Let me tell you what happened when Beth Roberts started wandering down the aisle, offering her box of home-made whole-wheat crackers left and right, to everyone.

"Oh, thanks," Mum said, taking two stuck together. "I'm absolutely starving."

Goggle-eyes fastidiously peeled the smallest one he could find away from its sticky companions.

"How nice," he said. "And how very unusual. Wheat-germ petits fours!"

You could tell from the look Beth gave him that she knew perfectly well he was being sarcastic. But just at that moment the bus began to slow. Everyone straightened up to look ahead over the seats in front. It seemed that we were coming up behind some vast great trailer with huge flashing WIDE LOAD signs, and a motorcycle escort.

"Look at the size of that!" breathed Beth. "What *is* it?" Suddenly a thought struck her. "I bet I can guess what it is," she said excitedly. "The nuclear convoys have to use this road." She craned her head to see better. "I bet it's one of them. It's absolutely *massive*. Yes, I bet this is part of a nuclear convoy."

Responding to signaling from the motorcycle escort, our bus was pulling out now, and drawing abreast of the wide load. Everyone had heard what Beth was saying. They all peered curiously out of the windows.

"Yes, indeed," Gerald Faulkner spoke into the

sudden silence as we saw the load clearly for the first time. "A lovely three-bedroomed nuclear missile with propane gas kitchen."

Beth flushed. Her mouth shut like a trap. As the immense mobile home on its trailer slipped away behind, she snapped the lid shut on her whole-wheat cracker box, and took off down the bus so fast she didn't offer one to Jude or me. I had to climb over Jude to go and get ours.

"Who *is* that fellow with your mother?" Beth asked. (She was still scarlet.)

I took a deep breath.

"He's my Mum's cousin," I lied. "Over from Perth."

She shrugged, appeased. Friends are one thing, relations are another. No one can blame their companions for flesh and blood.

"How long is he staying with you?" she asked, pressing an extra whole-wheat cracker in my hand for sympathy.

"Too long," I said. "Mum's very patient, though."

"Too patient," Beth said, and moved on down the bus, excusing Mum to everyone she passed. "He's some relation, it seems. Poor Rosie simply can't get rid of him. At her wit's end!"

Everyone nodded. They were all filled with sympathy. Even the ones at the back who couldn't see Goggle-eyes sneering had heard his loud snort of contempt when Josie sailed into the descant during the group's favorite song — "Three (-Two-One-

Bang!) Mile Island." They all knew how we were suffering.

I went back to my seat. As I clambered over her, Jude offered me one of the *Snoopy* books Mum bought her for the trip. (Jude is still bribed to come along, but Mum says I'm now old enough to do my civic duty without that). It turned out to be one I hadn't read. And though Beth's homemade whole-wheat crackers didn't taste too wonderful, reading and picking the sesame seeds out from between my teeth did help to pass the time till we arrived.

It was a pretty isolated place, where we stopped. I've been there several times. Apart from the miles of fencing, you can't see a thing. The base itself is in a dip behind thick woods. It didn't look as bleak as usual. For once the sun was glinting on the waters of the firth, and it wasn't misty. You could see bracken turning brown on the hills, and the heather was in flower.

Goggle-eyes clearly didn't like the look of the place much.

"I don't relish the thought of reclaiming that," he said, peering over Mum out of the window. "It looks pretty boggy."

He glanced out the other side.

"Look," he said. "Reinforcements."

Three dark-blue vans were waiting on a side road.

"Don't be so silly, Gerald," Mum said. "That's the police."

"Police?" He was astonished. "How come they're here before you even start?"

"They always arrive first," Mum said, pulling on her windbreaker and zipping it up. "They're more efficient than we are. If we say ten o'clock, they're here at ten o'clock, even if we don't turn up till eleven."

"You *tell* the police your plans?"

Mum stared at Goggle-eyes as if he'd just asked her whether she believed in fairies.

"Of *course* we tell them our plans," she said. "There are *dozens* of nuclear installations in Scotland. If we waited for the police to find us without help, we'd be here *weeks*."

Raising her eyes to heaven, she propelled him into the aisle.

We all piled off the bus, the smokers sighing with relief and fishing desperately in their jacket pockets. Beth strolled across to the police vans to find whoever was in charge, and all the rest of us followed the driver around to the back of the bus to get our stuff out of the luggage compartment.

I reached in for my banner. Goggle-eyes, being a gentleman, stretched over to take it from me as soon as he realised how long and unwieldy the poles were. But he didn't know that you have to keep the sheeting wrapped tightly if there's any wind at all. He let it loosen and, as the poles swung apart, it billowed open in the middle.

"What's this?" he said.

90

"It's just a banner," I said modestly.

It isn't "just a banner" at all. It took me and Grandma two whole weeks to make it, and it's one of the best. We have dozens of cardboard posters and homemade signs, but my banner's special. The only other good ones in the group are Beth's lovely quilted dove of peace, and the large fraying rainbow that we share with Greenpeace.

Mine is the biggest by far. Three meters wide and one high, you need two to carry it, marching abreast. It's hard to hold in strong winds — your hands ache terribly. But it's so striking that it's always worth it. I'll tell you what it's like. The sheet is white, and right across the top, painted in black letters, is

HOW TO DESTROY A WORLD

Right in the middle there's a plain white square, with one tiny black dot sitting all alone inside it. Then the whole of the rest of the banner is black dots — thousands and thousands of them — like the most awful case of measles.

Taking one of the poles out of his hand, I moved backward so that the banner unfurled, foot by foot. The wind whipped it taut, and Goggle-eyes saw the whole thing properly for the first time.

"What *is* it?" he asked again.

"It's my firepower banner."

"Firepower?"

"That's right." I pointed to the white space in the

center, to explain. "That little dot there, all by itself in the middle, represents all of the firepower used in the whole second world war."

"All of it? Every side?"

"All of it," I said. "From every country that was fighting. Three megatons of firepower."

"And all the rest?"

He waved his hand over the acres of measles.

"That's all the firepower in the nuclear weapons on the planet today."

"Dear gods!"

Poor Goggle-eyes looked a bit shattered.

"How many dots are there?" he asked after a moment. (That's everybody's next question.)

"Six thousand," I told him. "Exactly. Grandma helped me get it absolutely right. That's eighteen thousand megatons of firepower."

He whistled through his teeth.

"Six thousand second world wars," he said slowly.

"That's right."

Leave them to think, Mum says. Leave things to sink in at their own good speed. I stood holding my pole against the tug of the wind, and watched his eyes moving slowly over the banner. You can't just *look* at it. There are so many dots they swarm and jump. You get a headache if you stare too long. Grandma and I ought to know. We made it, and it nearly killed us.

Sure enough, after a moment he blinked and narrowed his eyes. But they kept moving over it.

"I'm going to roll it up again," I said after a bit. "Till we get going."

He watched me twist my pole until, foot by foot, the banner swallowed itself up. Then he stepped forward and took it from me.

"I'll grant you one thing," he said, slinging the poles over his shoulder and making off. "If all that ever goes up, there won't be much world left."

Raising my eyes to heaven, I followed him.

At the front of the bus, everyone was milling about impatiently.

"We really ought to get moving," Josie was saying. "Snowballing can take *hours*."

"Snowballing?" Mum looked confused. "I thought we were reclaiming hills."

"We were," said Josie. "Till Beth changed the plan last night. Now it seems we're snowballing instead."

A look of deep mystification settled on Gerald Faulkner's face. He stared up at the clear October skies, and you could tell exactly what he was thinking: *How can you snowball on a day like this?* He turned to Mum for an explanation, but she was already busy complaining to Josie:

"This snowballing is news to me. You can't expect people to turn up and snowball out of the blue!"

"Indeed, no." Gerald Faulkner supported Mum to the hilt. "No throwing snowballs on a day like this. Fat chance."

Everyone stared at him, including Mum. Now she, too, shook her head in disbelief and glanced up. You could tell exactly what she was thinking as well. *What is he talking about? How can you throw snowballs when there is no snow?*

It was Josie who enlightened Gerald Faulkner.

"Not *that* kind of snowball," she told him. "The *other* kind."

"What other kind?"

"Haven't you even *heard?*" She sighed. "Groups like ours are snowballing all over the country. Two people cut a fence, and the police arrest them. Next time it's four who do it. Then eight, sixteen, thirty-two, sixty-four — " She broke off. (I know from when she was group treasurer that mental arithmetic isn't her strong point.) "And so on," she finished up lamely. "More and more people, snowballing."

"But what's the *point?*" asked Goggle-eyes.

Everyone stared at him *harder,* if you see what I mean. If I hadn't been so busy pretending that he had nothing whatsoever to do with me, I'd have sunk my head into my hands out of pure shame.

"What do you mean, what's the point?" asked poor Josie.

Goggle-eyes spread his hands.

"Why do you *bother?*"

Now it was Josie's turn to be utterly baffled.

"Why do we bother to do *anything?*" she asked. "Why do we reclaim hills and collect signatures on petitions? Why do we march and hold silent candlelight vigils? Why do we write to politicians and wear our badges and send letters to the newspapers?"

She stopped and looked at Mum impatiently as if to say: "Honestly, Rosie! You brought this awful person. *You* explain!"

Mum tapped him on the shoulder.

"Gerald — "

He didn't notice. He was still persecuting Josie.

"But what's the point of getting yourselves *arrested?*"

"Listen," said Josie. "There are millions who think the way we do. *Millions.* People of all kinds. And this way the police and the courts and the newspapers get to see that we're not all the sorts of kooks and hippies who can be safely ignored. They get to see growing numbers of sensible citizens who *object* to these places. And from our statements in court, they get to hear *why.*"

"Then what?"

"You pay the fine. Or maybe you refuse on principle."

"And go to jail."

"Better than going to the lions," said Mum. "People have done that for their beliefs before now."

Gerald Faulkner fell silent. He looked around at all of us, staring back at him, and you could tell he thought that, apart from Jude who was still immersed in *Snoopy,* we were all totally unhinged. It was a bit of a relief when Beth came back.

As soon as I noticed who was following her over,

I nudged Jude in the ribs. Unwillingly, she lifted her eyes.

"What?"

"Look."

Jude looked. Her eyes lit up, and she closed the book for the first time since we arrived at the bus stop. Marching toward us was Inspector McGee, and she adores him. She's had a passion for him ever since we decorated the fence with flowers one Easter, and when she handed him a daffodil, he ate it. (I saw him. He ate the whole thing. He kept his face straight — well, straight as you can when you're munching a daffy — and he ate it right down to the bottom of the stalk. Now, of course, he is one of Jude's heroes.)

"Hello again," he said. He looked around for people he recognized, and when he noticed Jude, he winked. She went bright pink, and wriggled with pleasure. "You've picked a better day for it this time," he said.

He was dead right. Last time we had a demonstration in his territory, it sleeted in our faces all day long. We were all wretched, his officers were snarly and uncooperative, and the bus was even later than usual coming to pick us up. That was the day I distinctly overheard Mum telling Beth she'd sell her soul for a bomb to fall out of the sky and put us all out of our misery. (After a hot bath, of course, she flatly denied it.)

"Right, then," said Inspector McGee, rubbing his hands. "Who wants to be arrested today?"

He gave Jude a mock-hopeful look, and she shook her head, going all bashful on him, and sidling out of sight behind Gerald Faulkner's legs. There was a little bit of last-minute fussing, and then the snowballers stepped forward. Inspector McGee ran his eyes over them. You could tell he thought Beth's grandmother was far too old for this sort of thing, and the two boys from St. Serf's School were far too young. But he said nothing.

"Sixteen," Beth said proudly. "Twice as many as last time!"

He wasn't all that impressed. He'd brought more officers than that himself.

"To me, it's just twice the paperwork." He turned to the waiting snowballers and went all business-like.

"Now this is a brand-new fence," he warned. "No going berserk with the wirecutters. Only one strand each."

He turned to everybody else.

"I'm told the rest of you are just dying quietly."

This time Mum managed to step on Goggle-eyes' foot to shut him up before he even got his mouth open. She'd had enough of his embarrassing questions.

"That's right," she said. "The rest of us are just dying quietly."

Jude prodded Goggle-eyes.

"You'll *ruin* your suit," she warned him amiably. "Simon told Mum that just lying down and dying *once* turned his best jacket into a grubby rag."

"Lying down?" Along with this sudden enlightenment came pure horror. Goggle-eyes glanced at the waterlogged potholes all over the road. "I'm not lying down!"

"Not *here*," Jude comforted him. "Outside the main gates."

Goggle-eyes groaned. He groaned so deeply and sincerely that if I hadn't been standing there bubbling with anticipation, longing for him to ruin his best suit, I'd have felt sorry for him.

Mum sensed his gathering rebelliousness.

"Come on," she said to everyone. "Let's get moving. If we die quickly and they don't hang around at the fence, we could be home by teatime."

"I'll second that," said Inspector McGee. "My officers have got as cold as stones in the vans, waiting for you people."

Everyone started shuffling into place, raising cardboard signs and unfurling banners. Mum usually offers to hold one end of mine, but she was busy apologizing to Inspector McGee about the fact that, after all our promises last time, we'd been so late again. Jude, of course, trailed after the two of them like a besotted lamb. So when Gerald Faulkner sighed and reached out for the other pole, I let him take it. I thought, to be fair, that it was nice of him to offer, considering he's against practically everything the banner stands for. (Not that he needed to worry that anyone would see him. Apart from a few passing cars, and sheep watching curiously from the other side of the road, there was no one around. They don't shove these nuclear bases where you're going to see them, you know. They've got more sense than that. They might make you nervous.)

Just as we set off, a car full of servicemen spun around the corner. Leaning out of his window, the driver jeered loudly, and, as the car came past, deliberately steered the wheels through pools of rainwater on the side of the road, sending wet sheets of filth up in our faces.

"For God's sake!"

Goggle-eyes stared down at his sodden, splattered suit. His eyes narrowed, and there was one of his dangerous pauses. Then he swung around in time to see the back of the servicemen's car disappear around the next bend.

Well, you can't fight the armed forces, can you? Of course not. So he picked on us. Glowering at me, he waved his free hand to indicate the raggle-taggle procession ahead.

"You realize," he snarled, "that all these people would be far better off living under some form of dictatorship. They might no longer feel obliged to go around asserting their democratic rights!"

I lifted my side of the banner higher. It was his own fault. He should have taken Mum's advice, and worn a windbreaker and old shoes.

"In a dictatorship," I told him proudly, "all these people would probably already be dead."

And so, in perfect step if not in perfect accord, we followed everyone along the road toward the main gate of the submarine base.

Sighing, the police heaved themselves out of their vans and followed us.

6

✕✕✕

IT'S not as easy as you might think to get arrested. For one thing, there are never enough wire-cutters to go around.

"Who was supposed to bring the other pair?"

"That group from Muirglen. They said they'd meet the snowballers at the police station and provide transport home."

"What use is that? How will we ever get to the police station if we can't cut the wire?"

"This pair's completely blunt!"

"So are these!"

I blocked my ears against the bickering at the fence, stretched out, and stared up at the sky. When we do one of our die-ins, I let myself go all limp until the road no longer feels gritty and hard under my body. I lie and watch the clouds go scudding overhead, and try to forget that other people are packed around me like sardines, some grumbling that they've ended up in a puddle, some lost in thought, some coming out with those baffling snatches of conversation you always hear when you're close to strangers. Then, at a signal from whoever is organizing us, we quiet down to deathly and foreboding silence. However many times you've been a part of it, it still feels strange. Suddenly, with everyone lying there pretending, just for a few minutes, that the worst has actually happened, it's too late now, it's all over, the world seems larger, somehow, and more serious and more precious. And the police walkie-talkies suddenly sound so cheap and tinny and unimportant that some of the officers stare ahead in real embarrassment as the stupid chirruping pours from their jacket pockets.

Lie down and look up at the sky. It's such a small thing to do, but it makes such a difference. The sky looks so huge it's absolutely astounding. You only notice when you're flat on your back. Strolling along streets or glancing out of windows, you only get to see the thinnest rim of it. On your back, you can see it all: the vast upturned bowl that stretches miles and miles in peaceful blue, or hangs right over you in dark bruisy colors, threatening to spill. I think that everyone in the world should stretch out quietly for a while every single day of their lives, look up at the whole sky, and be astonished.

Our minutes of silence were over.

"I think that everyone should lie on their backs every day and stare up at the sky," I said. (It just popped out.)

"You must be *joking!*"

Goggle-eyes shuddered in horror and reached down from where he had been standing beside a couple of police officers, preserving what was left of his suit and his dignity. He hauled Mum to her feet.

"Kitty's right," Mum agreed, brushing grit off her jeans. "People waste too much of their lives rushing around building new things and pulling old things down. They ought to take time to look at what's been there forever."

"An empty sky!"

"Infinity," Mum corrected him. "Eternity."

Well, we can't all be closet philosophers. "Did you bring the sandwiches?" I interrupted, patting the bulging pockets of Mum's jacket. "I'm really hungry."

Unfortunately, this started Jude off.

"Me, too," she wailed. "When are we going ho-o-ome?"

"Please don't start whining," Mum told her irritably. "You know I can't stand it."

Jude didn't answer back. She never does. But, scowling, she sidled closer to Gerald Faulkner exactly the same way she always used to move toward Dad for his support whenever Mum was irritable. And, sure enough, Gerald immediately stuck up for her, just the way Dad always did.

"Go easy, Rosalind. It's been a tiring day."

Mum's like me. She hates people even *hinting* she might be being a bit unreasonable.

"For heaven's sake!" she snapped. "It hasn't been that bad! When I was young we used to have to sit for two whole hours every Sunday in a stone-cold church, bored stiff, to save our selfish little souls. Jude's lucky! A few times a year she gets a couple of hours of fresh air to try to save the whole world. Is that so terrible?"

There was a little Gerald Faulkner pause. I waited with interest. (It's not that often they're not directed at me.) Then:

"Do you know what you are, Rosalind?" he said. "You are almost *unbelievably* bossy."

Jude and I caught our breath. If Dad said anything like that, the fur would fly so fast, so furious, you'd hit the floor for safety. But, then again, Dad would have said it differently. It would have come out as a sort of snarl, a terrible insult. Somehow Gerald Faulkner managed to say it in an affectionate kind of way that made you think the fact that Mum was so bossy filled him with loving admiration.

And, astonishingly, that's the way she took it.

"I am bossy, aren't I?" she said. "Yes, I really am bossy."

I breathed again. So did Jude. I heard her.

"You're wasted running that hospital," Gerald Faulkner told Mum, as he ground the poles of my banner deep in the mud of the bank so it would stand up by itself. "You ought to be running the economy. Or the whole country! Or the world!"

Everyone around us, I noticed, was beginning to look rather uncomfortable now.

"Yes. I could run the world." Mum sounded keen.

"I'd do a really good job. I'd make an *excellent* dictator."

It was embarrassing. She honestly didn't seem to notice that half the people who overheard were reaching down for the little waterproof backpacks that held their thermos bottles and banana yogurts, and were edging away uneasily. Others were standing paralyzed, with their mouths full of alfalfa-sprout sandwiches, watching with shocked expressions.

Goggle-eyes didn't seem to notice either. Or, if he did, he didn't care.

"You'd be ideal!" he assured her. "You have the basic qualification for the job. You know for a simple fact that, to be absolutely in the right, people need do no more than come around to your views."

"He's right," Mum told the few people who could still bear to remain in earshot. "He's absolutely right!"

I made a solemn vow right then and there to change my name, dye my hair, and join another group. Like everyone else, I started shuffling away, pretending to take a sudden interest in what was happening up at the fence where the snowballers were still grinding away ineffectually at their chosen strands of wire, and an assortment of police officers were standing by, eyeing the rain clouds ominously gathering on the horizon, and patiently waiting to make their arrests.

The snowballers kept up a constant chatter as they toiled away.

"Could I have a turn with your wire-cutters after you've finished?"

"These are no good. I thought I might try yours."

"These? These are useless!"

One of the policewomen shifted restlessly, and looked at her watch. It was clear she was dying to get back to the station. Inspector McGee squinted up at the clouds as they rolled steadily nearer. The other officers contented themselves with exchanging meaningful glances while the snowballers hacked away at the wire. It was obvious what they were thinking. "Thank God these people aren't defending the country!" I know because they had exactly the same look on their faces as Goggle-eyes did, except that he, of course, had made a point of saying it out loud, several times, till even Jude got bored with hearing it, and wandered off along the line of snowballers to see who was doing the best. She came to a dead halt halfway along, beside Fish Eyes, like a supermarket shopper who has finally worked out which checkout is likely to be free first, and, sure enough, after a moment there was a rustle of excitement where she was standing.

"Mine's coming! I think mine's coming! Yes!"

And, seconds later, from Grubby Green Jacket:

"I've done it, too! I'm through the wire!"

The first two to succeed punched the air in triumph, and grinned. The police officers sighed, and a couple of them moved forward.

"Off we go, then."

"Fine."

Still smiling proudly, Fish Eyes and Grubby Green Jacket were led off toward the open doors of the blue vans. Everyone else turned their attention back to the fence.

"Who's next?"

"Try the hacksaw."

"Press harder!"

"Don't press so hard!"

"How can a strand of wire this thin turn out to be so *tough?*"

We cheered as, one by one, the snowballers completed their task and were led off to the police vans. Beth's grandmother cheated. She let a pregnant woman in pink dungarees do all her cutting for her. All that Beth's grandmother did was lay her hacksaw on the broken strand, and claim loudly and dishonestly:

"I've done it! I have cut the wire!"

Graciously, Inspector McGee turned a blind eye to the deception. Pink Dungarees looked far too pregnant to spend long in a police station, and anyway, Inspector McGee knows better than to tangle with Beth's grandmother. As usual, she slid her arm in his, and made him escort her personally back to the vans, carrying her comfy peace cushion. Everyone grinned as she hobbled by on his arm. She gets away with it every time. I've seen her forcing even the sullen and unpleasant police officers to be helpful and polite as they arrest her. Mum says it only works because she's so old. Mum says they know she can remember back when they were truly there to oblige the people, and not just the paramilitary arm of the state that they've become today. Being reminded of how much things have changed makes them uneasy, Mum says, so they treat her properly.

The rain clouds were rolling nearer and nearer, but the advice we shouted to each snowballer was getting better with experience, so the arrests were coming quicker now. Soon there were only three snowballers left at the fence. Flowery Headscarf from St. Thomas and St. James got the only good pair of wire-cutters. Delaying for only a couple of moments, smiling, while someone from her church group took a photograph, she snapped her strand through cleanly, cheered herself, and then without thinking handed the wire-cutters to the policewoman standing beside her.

"Hey!"

The last two snowballers looked up from their strands of wire. One was the shy wind-power engineer to whom, earlier in the day, Gerald Faulkner had been complaining about windmills. The other was a student called Ben, who once spent a whole bus ride to Edzell airbase trying to help Simon explain decimals to Jude.

"Excuse me," the wind-power engineer said to the policewoman. "We need those. These are useless."

It was the same policewoman who had been looking at her watch. Now she looked at the wire-cutters that had ended up in her hand, and said, exasperated beyond measure:

"But I can't give them back now!"

The engineer was too shy to argue. He shrugged

and turned back to the fence. But Ben didn't give up so easily. (Anyone who can try and explain decimals to Jude can't be a quitter.) Pushing his fingers backward through his hair, he tried to wheedle his way around the officer.

"Oh, go on," he tempted her. "We'll be here hours otherwise. This pair's quite blunt."

He took care to glance up at the huge purple cloud that now hung over all our heads.

You should have seen the look on the policewoman's face. She was in torment. She glanced at her watch a second time, then back at the wire-cutters. You could tell she was kicking herself for allowing her fingers to close around the handles of the stupid things in the first place. And, to make matters worse, one or two heavy drops of cold rain splattered down, threatening all of us still standing waiting, but not those safely seated in the vans, ready to go.

"But I can't hand back wire-cutters accidentally in my possession so you can do criminal damage!"

"We're going to cut the wire anyhow. This way we'll just do it quicker."

"Much quicker," agreed the engineer, still sawing away at the fence, getting nowhere.

The policewoman looked over at her colleague still standing behind the engineer, waiting to arrest him. He wasn't much help to her. He just stared back blankly. So she looked around for Inspector McGee. But he, of course, was still out of sight behind the vans, no doubt settling Beth's grandmother on her comfy peace cushion and exchanging hairy old Scottish Ban the Bomb March reminiscences.

Ben shrugged, and turned back to the fence.

"This will take hours," he threatened.

The policewoman suddenly made up her mind. With a flash of decisive thinking that Mum said later was a tribute to her training, she flipped the only good pair of wire-cutters into the grass.

"Whoops!" she said. "Dropped them!"

The engineer and Ben dived together. Ben, being younger and fitter, got to them first. Swooping them up with one hand, he passed her his useless pair with the other.

"Allow me," he said courteously, as though he were simply handing her back the pair she had dropped.

"Thank you," she murmured.

"And thank *you*."

He swung around on the fence. I think his big mistake must have been to go at the wire as forcefully as if he still had the blunt pair he was using before. He certainly did something stupid. I'm sure if he'd been handling them properly they'd never have slipped like that and pinched his finger so horribly.

"Ow! Ow-*ow*-OW!"

Again the wire-cutters fell in the grass. Sucking his finger, poor Ben jumped up and down, yelping with pain.

"Ow-*ee!* It hurts!"

"Let me see." The policewoman looked anxious.

Ben put out his hand and slowly, gingerly, extended his fingers. You could see where the wire-cutter handle had pincered his finger. On either side were the sort of drained patches of squashed skin you know are going to turn straight into massive black bruising as soon as the blood can bring itself to flow back.

"Oh, that is nasty!" said the policewoman.

"Poor Ben," said Jude, and her eyes filled with sympathetic tears. She's quiet, Jude is, but she's loyal. She never forgets anyone in the ever-growing army of those who've helped her with her arithmetic homework.

Behind us, alerted by the howls of pain, Mum tore herself away from offering Goggle-eyes the job of grand vizier in her despotic regime, and scrambled up the bank to take a peek at the damage. Mum's good with accidents. She's got that perfect mix of being both calm and — well, yes, he's quite right — almost unbelievably bossy.

"Show me," she ordered him. And when he had: "Oh, that is nasty!" she echoed the policewoman. (Two real professionals.)

Ben didn't respond to these sophisticated diagnoses. Poor soul looked pale as a maggot. I think he was about to faint.

The policewoman turned to Gerald, who had been scrambling up the bank after Mum and now stood gasping for breath at her side.

"Would you help me get this young man to the bus before he keels over?"

She must have chosen Gerald because of what was left of his nice suit. She couldn't have picked him because of his physical fitness. He was still panting heavily as he obediently took Ben's other arm to support him.

Ben tried to shake them off.

"I'm not going to the bus," he insisted. "I'm going in the vans. I'm being arrested."

"No, you're not," Mum said. "That's going to turn into the most unpleasant bruise. You're going home."

She turned to the policewoman for support, and the policewoman clinched it.

"I wouldn't arrest you anyway," she declared baldly. "You never even got through your bit of fence."

You could tell everyone thought this was a bit harsh. One or two of the Quakers looked a little reproachful, and Ben was positively outraged. But Gerald and the policewoman cut short his indignant protests by leading him off firmly toward the bus. As they stumbled past me down the muddy slope, I heard Ben muttering darkly about conspiracies; but apart from gripping his arm just that little bit tighter, and speeding up, the policewoman and Gerald simply ignored him.

While the engineer was still snipping gingerly at his own stubborn strand of fence wire, Mum looked around the little knot of bystanders. As usual she seemed to have completely taken over.

"We need one more now," she announced. "A replacement for Ben. Any volunteers?"

Silence. To make the point that whoever was going to volunteer had better get a move on, a few more drops of cold rain fell. Everyone glanced at one another with those helpless little I-would-if-I-could shrugs.

"Come on," cajoled Mum. "It's only a couple of hours down at the station. Your court case won't come up for weeks."

Everyone took a sudden interest in their muddy toe-caps.

"We need another person," Mum insisted. "This snowball is going to look pathetic if we don't even have sixteen."

I don't know how they held out against her, truly I don't. I cracked.

"I'll do it."

"Certainly not!"

Then even Jude began to look a little bit wistful. She opened her mouth once or twice, daring herself to volunteer. But even her passion for Inspector McGee couldn't triumph over her tiredness, and the fact that her feet were cold, and the unknown territory of "down at the station." And Mum would only have ignored her anyway. So we all stood there looking terribly uncomfortable, while the last policeman carefully kept his face straight, and Mum's eyes roved over everyone just like Mrs. Lupey's do when she's waiting for someone in the class to confess to some heinous crime like dropping a chocolate wrapper on the floor, or sliding the window down a micromillimeter while she's turned her back to write something on the black-board.

But these people aren't so easily intimidated. After all, if they cared all that much what others thought of them, they wouldn't have come along on the demonstration in the first place. So they just kept on politely inspecting the ends of their shoes, and I honestly believe that, but for what happened next, the whole business might have been wrapped up with a few more moments of stern waiting, and then Mum shrugging and breaking the silence with something like: "Oh, well. Fifteen. Sixteen. What's the difference?"

But the policeman snorted.

Personally, I would have ignored it. After all, if Gerald Faulkner had been standing there, he probably would have snorted too, and just as loudly. But, let's face it, Mum's soft on Goggle-eyes. She wasn't soft on the policeman.

"Lost your tissues?" she asked him in exactly the same tone of voice Grandma uses for "Had your eyeful?" And I told you already that that sounds so rude Mum's ordered me and Jude to stop saying it, ever.

It irritated him, you could tell, her coming back at him like that. And he was pretty young. Maybe Mum's scornful response reminded him of being scolded by his own mother for tracking mud from his regulation boots over her nice clean floors or something. Anyway, suddenly he got exactly the same sort of look all over his face that Jude gets when she's fed up with Mum. And he muttered sullenly:

"Make up your minds! Fifteen or sixteen. I can't have you wasting any more of my time."

He put his foot right in it there.

"*Your* time! What about *mine?*" (Even if she hadn't before, I bet she sounded like his mother now.) "This is your *job,* you know! You're *paid* to do it." Mum shook her finger at him as if he were about three, or something. "I'm a lot busier than you are, you know. And my job is equally as important as yours. Not only that, but I have two children to care for, and a house to run. You'd better not tell me I'm wasting *your* time. I am a lot more bothered about wasting my own!"

I must say, Inspector McGee must do a really good job of training his officers. I'd have been terribly tempted to arrest her for nagging. But maybe he realized that, if he did, we'd have the satisfaction of making up the full number we wanted. So, whether it was an admirable example of highly trained self-control, or just simple petty-minded spite, he somehow managed not to respond. He just stared straight ahead, as if he were a thousand miles away, and stone deaf.

Mum was just on the verge of opening her big mouth to start in on him again when Gerald, back within earshot after his errand of mercy, realized what was going on. Practically throwing himself up the last few slippery feet of the bank, he caught her arm.

"Now stop it, Rosalind!" he warned. "It's not the officer's fault you've spent all day here."

"It's not my fault, either," she responded irritably.

"I know which I'd prefer between spending a nice quiet Sunday at home with my feet up, secure in the knowledge that we had a sane defense policy" — she waved her arms about — "and this!" She could have been indicating anything: the mud or the occasional stinging splatters of rain, the unsightly fence stretching for miles in either direction or the bedraggled company. "Dragging around bleak military outposts, carrying rain-soaked signs and trailing my poor little toddlers behind me!"

I ignored "poor little toddlers." I took it to be what Mrs. Lupey always calls "a rather unfortunate rhetorical flourish." But Jude, I noticed, looked extremely hurt. Once again, she moved so close to Gerald Faulkner that she practically stuck to his mud-streaked trousers. From this safe vantage point, she glowered at Mum.

So did the police officer. But you could tell he was determined not to be drawn into some interminable wrangle about effective ways of influencing government defense policy from the grass roots. Gritting his teeth, he only muttered:

"Can we just go now? All fifteen?"

It wasn't *that* sarcastic. I was *there*. I *heard* it. At the most, he stressed "fifteen" the tiniest, tiniest bit. Mum claims he curled his lip like a theatrical villain and actually sneered it. But all the rest of us agreed later that, in the circumstances of her hectoring him in front of everyone as if he personally had refitted

116

every nuclear submarine in Britain, he'd shown quite admirable restraint.

More than she did, anyway. I know she hates sarcastic people — she's like me — but, frankly, she must have temporarily gone unhinged to act the way she did when he said "fifteen." Shaking off Gerald, she dived headlong into the grass beside the fence. Then, snatching up the good pair of wire-cutters still lying there, she forced open the handles and, before we had time to realize what she was doing, with one deft wrench she snipped a strand of the fence wire.

"Sixteen!"

Everyone cheered. Well, the Quakers started it, of course, because they're always so very nice and encouraging about everything. But everyone else joined in, even Jude. And it was only me and Gerald Faulkner who were left standing absolutely horrified, watching in silence.

Then Mum realized what she'd done. She turned to me, as appalled as I was.

"Oh, Kitty!" she said. "I'm so sorry!"

I put a brave face on it. There wasn't much else I could do. The policeman was already bearing down on Mum.

"It's all right," I told her. "It doesn't matter. It's only a couple of hours down at the station. Your court case won't come up for weeks."

Mum had the grace to blush. She turned to Jude. "Sweetheart?"

Jude looked bewildered. I think my saying the words "down at the station" had taken a bit of the gloss off the excitement of clapping along with everyone else. But even so, she hadn't truly caught on that Mum had actually managed to get herself arrested.

Gerald stepped forward, and laid a protective hand on Jude's shoulder. He looked absolutely livid with Mum. His tone, when he spoke to her, was steely with disapproval.

"I shall, of course, look after both your girls till you get back."

Apart from the fact that his suit was splattered and streaked all over with fresh mud, he looked and sounded just like one of those straightlaced solicitors in old Victorian serials on television. But Jude didn't even seem to notice his grim tones. She just looked up at him rather gratefully when he said this, and slid her hand in his.

Mum said rather nervously:

"I won't be long, honestly. I'll be back before you know it."

The policeman took her arm.

"Don't bank on it," he warned. "We're short-staffed, and there are twice as many of you as last time."

He meant it as a sort of threat, you could tell. But it had quite the opposite effect on Mum, of course. It cheered her up.

"We did it!"

There was a ragged ripple of applause, and a few

tired cheers. Even the nice Quakers wanted to pack it in now, and head home.

Mum was led off, toward the vans. All the way there, she kept leaning back, giving me silly orders and instructions. I was to remember to switch off the grill after I made toast. I wasn't to leave my electric blanket on after I put out my light. There were some cans of soup on the top shelf of the pantry. Honestly, you'd think I'd never even visited our house before, let alone lived there.

"For heaven's sake!" Gerald told Mum sharply. "Stop fussing, Rosalind. Kitty is perfectly capable, and I shall be there!"

I think Inspector McGee must have sent his officers to a course for avoiding domestic violence. The young policeman swung open the door of the blue van as quickly as he could. Everyone already seated inside cheered Mum.

"Sixteen!"

"Well done, Rosie!"

"Come on up!"

Mum turned before clambering inside.

"Thanks, Gerald," she said. You could tell she was desperate for him to soften and give her just one brief smile of encouragement before the van drove off. But she'd picked the wrong man.

"Don't mention it," he said icily as she scrambled inside. "*Somebody* has to act responsibly."

That got her. She stopped fishing for sympathy and support, and went all defiant.

"Oh, shut up, Gerald!" she snapped. "What could be more irresponsible than passively sitting back while half-baked politicians and trigger-happy generals cling to a defense policy that means every child on the planet could end up frying alive!"

And she swung the van door closed herself — right in his face.

I was so proud of her. That shut him up.

Behind us, everyone burst into song. While the last couple of officers checked the van doors and then walked around to take their own seats, we all sang to the snowballers inside. We sang "We Shall Overcome," and I started crying. I always cry when we sing that. Mum says that that's because the song is true, and we *shall* overcome one day. She says the song's been sung through more than one just cause, and in the end the singers have been able to hang up their hats, and go home satisfied. Our day will come, she says. Just be strong and patient.

Then, as the rain began to fall in earnest, the vans drew away, splashing mud out of the potholes. Everyone except Gerald waved like mad, even after they were quite sure that no one in the vans could see any longer. They all kept singing too, but I didn't bother. I wanted to leave. Jude was all right. She was still standing beside Gerald, holding his hand tight, and looking completely unruffled. But I didn't feel too cheerful myself. I wasn't worried, exactly; but I felt shaky. It's not so nice to watch your mother being driven off by the police, especially when your dad lives a hundred miles away.

The song was ending, but I couldn't stop the tears. It didn't matter, though. The rain was beating down so hard now, no one could really tell. But I turned away anyhow, just in case, and scrambled down the bank for the last time.

Uprooting my banner, I slung the two poles together over my shoulder, and trudged off down the road on my own, toward the bus.

Gerald was right. It had been a tiring day. And I'd had enough.

7

×××

I'D only been slumped in the bus seat for a couple of minutes before he disturbed me.

"Would you move over and make room for me and Judith?"

Make room? There had been loads of free seats on the bus when we arrived. Now there were even more, with sixteen fewer people traveling back with us. But clearly Gerald Faulkner expected me to shift across to the window, and give him my seat. I can't say I rushed to cooperate. I opened my eyes, though.

"Can't you sit there?" I waved toward the double seat in front.

"Slide over," he insisted. "I think right now your sister probably needs both of us."

Only a few weeks before I would have argued. I would have responded tartly: "Do you? I think she probably just needs me." But now I didn't. I thought about it — practically opened my mouth to snap it out — but, frankly, I didn't really think that it was true any more. Poor Jude was standing there looking wiped out. Her thumb was in her mouth (for once he wasn't telling her to take it out again) and she was staring fixedly at me. But she was leaning against his legs, and she was still holding his hand very tightly.

I moved across. He took my place and gathered Jude into his arms. She sprawled across him with her legs on me. It was a bit of a squash, but not uncomfortable. Jude slid her thumb out of her mouth just long enough to reach across the aisle and pick a crumpled newspaper off the seat cushion.

"Read to me," she ordered.

He slid his arm further around her, to open the paper. I watched with interest. He could have chosen to read to her about a massive fight in a public lavatory in the Tottenham Court Road. Or the mysterious midnight explosion of a furniture-polish factory in Wrexham. Or the woman suing a posh French restaurant because she found chunks of stewed carpet in her *crème brûlée*. But no, not him. He chose to read Jude the "Review of the Week's Business News."

"Shares continued their steady revival with the FT-SE share index finishing the week improving 33.2 points to 1,750.2," he droned. "The FT-30 share index gained 27.3 points to 1,405.1, crossing the 1400 points line for the first time in two months. Gold shares improved by up to three quarters of a million pounds . . ."

She wasn't listening, of course. She was asleep.

He slept, too, after a bit. His head rolled back. His

glasses slid a little down his nose, and he made this soft sort of rustling noise through his lips as he breathed, like papers on a desk stirred by the breeze. From time to time Jude thrashed around a bit in her sleep, but it didn't seem to bother him. He just slid his arms more tightly around her till she settled again, murmuring something soothing in her ear, and patting whichever bit of her lay under his hand. He didn't even bother to open his eyes. And as we pulled into the main street of our hometown, I realized Jude had stayed fast asleep in his arms for the whole journey. I'm not spiteful about old Goggle-eyes on principle, you know. Even I can give credit where it's due, and it was due that afternoon. He can be really kind and fatherly when he tries.

And he can be really bossy and fatherly, too. He was that way when we got back. Admittedly he'd promised Mum that he'd look after us for her, but you'd think that he actually owned us, the way he went on. He wouldn't let us do what we usually do after a demonstration, and pick up supper from the McDonald's on the corner. (Mum always lets us. She says she reckons political activity may be psychologically inspiriting but it's physically enfeebling, and she couldn't possibly come home and *cook*.) Gerald dragged us bodily past McDonald's, and ended up going through the kitchen with a toothcomb, looking for something "sensible." That was the word he used. He turned down all Jude's suggestions for quick and easy things to eat — ice cream, frozen party sausage rolls, fried bananas — on the grounds that they just weren't sensible, and sent her upstairs with a lump of cheese and an apple to keep her going while she had her bath.

I stayed in the kitchen doorway, nibbling the chunk of cheese he'd given me, and found myself pressed into peeling potatoes.

"Can't we have frozen french fries?"

"No, we can't! It was a strenuous day, and both of you need something sensible, and then an early night."

"Can't we stay up for Mum?"

He paused, trimming the fat off some pork chops he'd found in the fridge.

"You can," he told me. "Judith can't."

He's odd that way. He never seems to have the least trouble making decisions. Poor Mum could never say a thing like that straight out. She'd hum and haw, and try to wriggle out of it with stupid little sayings, like "We'll see" and "Let's wait and find out how it goes." And if Jude started arguing that it wasn't fair that she should be sent up to bed earlier just because she's younger, Mum would tie herself in the most terrible knots trying to persuade her to agree, without directly ordering her around.

Ordering us around is no problem for Goggle-eyes. If Jude came down and tried to argue with him, all she'd get would be: "Because you're younger, that's why." Or even: "Because I say so." I could have made a fuss. But, after all, he'd said I could stay up. And anyway, you only had to look at Jude to see she was exhausted. So I said nothing and just kept on working away at the sink, peeling the mucky spuds. And suddenly, like a reward from heaven for my self-restraint, his arm appeared at my side with one of those smashing ice-tinkling, tonic-fizzing, lemon-swirling drinks of his.

"Cheers!" he said.

He's absolutely right. There's something really *cheerful* about these sparkling drinks he puts in your hand. Even the glasses look brighter than all the rest in the cupboard, as if he'd polished them till they glittered on a tea towel before even starting to put anything in them. And it was nice of him to go to all the trouble of making me one anyway, even though Mum wasn't there. I knew he'd done it especially because, when I turned around, I saw he'd chosen something completely different for himself. So he had sliced the lemon and dug out the ice cubes and fetched the tonic bottle just for me.

"Cheers!" I said. "Thanks very much." And I nearly said "Gerald," except I thought he might have noticed and I might have blushed.

Supper was fun, when we finally got around to eating it. (He sent Jude back upstairs twice before he would serve the food: once for her bathrobe, and once for her furry slippers.) We didn't have to worry, either, about keeping enough for Mum. He filled a heatproof dish with hers, and put it in the oven to keep warm.

"There," he said firmly. "Now what's left on the table is all ours."

You wouldn't believe how many potatoes I ate that evening. I must have been halfway starving to death. Even Jude finished off her peas and ate two thick slices of bread and butter on top of everything else. We chewed and chewed, and it was only after half the food had disappeared that we got around to talking.

Goggle-eyes started it.

"Do you want to know what I think?" he asked me suddenly, fork aloft.

Normally I'd have made a face that said "No thanks, I don't," even if I reluctantly murmured, "Yes. Tell me." But I was curious.

"What do you think?"

He dabbed his mouth with a napkin he'd found in the bottom of a drawerful of stuff that was going to Goodwill.

"Frankly, I think all you scruffy people give the antinuclear movement a really bad name."

Good thing I had a mouthful of pork chop! He got a chance to explain before I could start yelling at him.

"Listen," he said. "You people ought to dress better. You ought to change things around. Look at your mother. She goes off to work at the hospital every morning looking elegant and respectable, but does she wear her little antinuclear badge? No, she doesn't. So no one who ever meets her during the day thinks: 'What a nice, responsible woman that is. She was so kind and helpful to me. She seems like a splendid citizen, and I bet she's a wonderful mother. But, imagine! She's wearing one of those little antinuclear badges. She must be a member of the antinuclear movement. So they can't all be the misinformed troublemakers and ne'er-do-wells the papers often make out!' "

I'd swallowed, but I didn't interrupt. It seemed to me what he was saying made some kind of sense.

"Then, take today," he went on. "She leaves all those stylish work clothes in the wardrobe, and puts on shapeless woollen clothes that look as if they came out of a charity box. She chooses shoes that look as if they were specifically designed to kick policemen on the shins, and wears a jacket that would disgrace a tramp. And then she proudly pins on her antinuclear badge!"

Put like that, he did seem to have a point.

"But you've got to stay warm," I argued. "It's chilly work."

"You're all prepared to suffer for your beliefs," he said. "I've seen you. Today was without a doubt the most tedious and boring and uncomfortable Sunday I've spent in *years*. It's just a matter of trading off one miserable discomfort against another. You'd be a little less protected against the weather, but you'd be more protected against the sneers." He shook his fork at me (which wasn't like him). "If you all dressed like lawyers and doctors and solicitors, you'd find your-selves treated with a whole lot more respect. Besides,"

128

he added, "you could always use some of your campaign funds to buy collective thermal underwear."

I shuddered. The idea of sharing an undershirt and long johns with some of the people who come on our demonstrations was pretty revolting.

"Another thing," he said, reaching out to correct Jude, who was holding her fork wrong. "Why go to out-of-the-way holes where only the sheep can see you? It's crazy. You ought to be outside government offices on weekdays, or in shopping centers on Saturday mornings. At least then a few people would get to read what it says on your banners before you're carted off to the nearest police station."

I didn't answer that one. I didn't know how. I've often thought myself that the sheep in the west of Scotland must be the most politically informed sheep in the world.

"And if you must go out to the middle of nowhere, why waste time singing silly songs? You should get organized. Someone should bring stamps, and someone paper, and you should spend your journey writing letters to your Member of Parliament, and the Prime Minister, and all the local papers, explaining exactly what you're all doing, and why."

There's no denying it. He was absolutely right.

"Three (-Two-One-Bang!) Mile Island!" He snorted with contempt again, just as he had on the bus ride. "Pure, self-indulgent rubbish! The time spent singing would have been far better employed writing to the Director of the Nuclear Inspectorate expressing your concern at the rising incidence of childhood leukemia around nuclear installations!"

"You ought to be on our side," I told him.

"Certainly not!" He shuddered. "I don't approve at all!"

"Then why pass out these handy hints?"

He shook his head. "I can't help it," he told me. "I'm a small-businessman. I can't bear inefficiency. Wherever I see it, I want to root it out." He glowered suddenly. "And I can't bear rudeness, either. I shall be writing to the commander of that submarine base complaining about the mischievous behavior of men supposedly under his command." The glower deepened to a thorough scowl. "My suit is *ruined*."

He did sound a bit like Simon, I must admit. But, still, it wasn't tactful of Jude to giggle.

"Finished?" he asked her, noticing her empty plate. And then he laid a heavy hand on her shoulder. "You must be tired out. I think you'd better go straight up to bed just as soon as you've finished helping with the dishes."

"You must be joking," I said. "Jude never helps with the dishes."

(I couldn't help it. It's a very sore point.)

His hand slid off her shoulder. "Never helps? Why not?" He looked at her enquiringly, saying to me: "She's got arms, hasn't she? She can reach in the sink."

Jude began edging off toward the door, making the most of her silent furry slippers.

I shrugged.

"I suppose it's just because she's so much younger," I told him.

Gerald stared.

"That is the silliest thing I ever heard," he said. "By that reasoning, the youngest child in every family in Scotland would reach adulthood without the faintest notion of how to make with the mop and the Ivory Liquid."

It's no more than the truth. I've said the same often enough myself. It's just that, at this point, Jude always puts on her pathetic little waif face, and Mum is wracked with guilt and says something like: "Oh, well. Maybe tomorrow. But I'll take a turn for her tonight since she's not very good at it."

Gerald was obviously immune to the pathetic little waif face. But, with him clearly taking up the part I usually played with such enthusiasm, for some extraordinary reason I took up Mum's part.

"She could do the breakfast dishes instead," I suggested. "She won't be quite so tired then."

Jude stopped her silent shuffle toward the door.

"She's not so tired now," Gerald insisted. "She's not as tired as I am, for example. I cooked the meal. And she's not as tired as you are. You peeled the potatoes. And she slept for two whole hours on the bus."

He turned to Jude. During this speech, she'd shuffled the last few feet toward the door, but she hadn't quite summoned up enough courage to disappear through it. I think she sensed that, unlike Mum, he'd just come after her and fetch her back.

"Would you like a stool to stand on?" he asked her politely. "Or can you reach?"

I was still nervous, I don't know why. Maybe it was the outraged look on Jude's face.

"Can't we just leave the dishes till morning?" I asked. (Another of Mum's great standby lines.)

"No," Gerald said. "No, we cannot. Only slatterns and drunks leave the dishes till morning."

(I made a mental note to tell Mum this.)

"Anyway," he added. "You're only trying to protect your sister. You are as bad as your mother in that respect. And Judith doesn't need your help, you know. Everyone around here treats her as if she were still a baby, but in fact she is perfectly capable."

Now that was *definitely* my line. If I've said that once, I've said it well over a thousand times. I had my mouth wide open when he turned to Jude.

"Aren't you?" he demanded.

Jude narrowed her eyes. It was a toss-up, I reckoned, between heart-rending sobs and roof-raising temper. But I was wrong. The fact is that, for some reason or other best known to herself, our Jude simply adores old Goggle-eyes, and in her book the man can do no wrong. If he says she's not tired, then she's not tired. If he says she can do the dishes, then she can.

"Yes," she said firmly. "And I don't need a stool. I can reach."

"That's my girl," Gerald said. "I knew you could do it!"

I was left speechless, honestly I was. When someone else steals your lines, what can you say?

She did the whole pile by herself. He told her how — glasses first; silverware next; then dishes; last, the greasy pans. She toiled away, having a bit of trouble with the stacking, but Gerald kept his nerve, and in the end she got through without any accidents at all. She looked really proud of herself when she hung up the apron.

After she'd finished, he inspected it. (I'm not kidding. He actually came across and picked up a couple of forks and peered at them closely, then held up one or two glasses to the light.)

"Well done," he said. "From now on you can do them every other night. Is that all right with you?"

"Fine," she said, grinning proudly. I nearly fainted. I must have been trying to wrangle a deal halfway as fair as that for *five whole years.*

"All right, then," he said. "That's settled. And now, as a reward, I shall come upstairs with you and read you a story."

He may, or may not, have read her the story first, I don't know. It was at least ten minutes before I went up there. But when I walked past, on my way to the bathroom, it wasn't a story he was reading to her, that was for sure. I heard the soothing rumble of his voice right from the top of the stairs.

"Higher-rate taxpayers, like nontaxpayers, have to

take care they get the best from their savings. For both, tax-free investments such as Personal Equity Plan, Save as You Earn schemes, and friendly-society investments are all attractive. Because of this, of course, the Inland Revenue sets very strict limits on how much can be invested — "

I peeped in. He was propped up against her pillows, his legs stretched out on her coverlet. He'd kicked his shoes off on the bedside rug. She lay comfortably in the crook of his arm, listening in rapt attention as he read to her from the Ross & Killearn Building Society Step-by-Step Guide to Good Money Management that came free with her big plastic acorn money box.

He came down ten minutes later, triumphantly flicking off unnecessary lights.

". . . seven, eight, nine! There! That should slow the little electric wheel down to a sprint!"

I followed him into the living room. I had to. It was practically pitch-dark now all over the rest of the house. Before he even noticed I was behind him, he'd stepped across and flicked the television switch as well. With perfect timing, "Scots Money Box" appeared on the screen.

I sat beside him on the sofa. After he'd been so nice and cooked our supper, and saved me from doing half the dishes for the next ten years, it seemed rude to sit miles away in the armchair.

"Don't you ever get bored with all this stuff?" I asked him.

134

"Stuff?" he said. "What stuff?"

I nodded toward the television. Ms. Moira Mc-Cready was warning everyone in Scotland that they should think very hard indeed about the new retirement options.

"This stuff. Don't you ever find it the slightest bit boring?"

"Dear me, no." It seemed to be the first time the idea had struck him. "Not boring, no. Not at all boring."

His answer interested me.

"You don't think it's a bit of a boring way of looking at the lovely green planet you live on?"

A spot of pink rose on his cheeks. I think he thought I might be needling him. But I was taking the greatest care not to seem hostile or aggressive or contemptuous. I truly wanted to know. His eyes shifted from me to Ms. Moira McCready on the TV going on and on about the advantages of the new Earnings-Related Retirement Plans, and finally he answered:

"It's just the way I've always thought about things."

I took even more care now. Casually picking at a loose thread in my sock, I asked him politely:

"But, Gerald." (Yes! I said it!) "Suppose you looked around you one day really hard, and suddenly had a sort of vision. Suppose you saw the trees and skies and clouds and birds and animals as clearly as if you were seeing them for the first time, and realized you maybe only had a hundred years to live on the

135

planet, and make the most of them all, and be happy. Wouldn't you think, after that vision, whenever you were reading the stock exchange reports or mutual fund handbooks, that maybe the way you think about things is — well — a little bit boring?"

(I meant thin, miserable, unimaginative, blind, even stupid! But, being polite, I said "boring.")

However carefully I wrapped the question up, I still thought he might find it rude. But I wanted to know the answer, I honestly did. It suddenly occurred to me that part of the reason I'd found it so difficult to get along with Goggle-eyes was that he was so different from me and Mum, and thought and cared about such different things. And suddenly I thought, if I could only *understand,* I might be able to get along with him better.

However offensive the question may have appeared to him, he didn't seem cross. He gave it quite a bit of thought while Ms. Moira McCready burbled on about additional voluntary contributions, and death-in-service cover, and alternative options. And then he finally came out with it — his explanation.

"Maybe it's just because I really am boring myself. I think I might be. Sometimes I look at people like you and your mother, and I think: 'No, I was never like that, even when I was young.' Maybe I was born boring. Maybe I was boring in my cradle."

His eyes were still watching Ms. Moira McCready opening and shutting her mouth, but he no longer heard her. He wasn't just politely answering me now. He was telling me something that mattered to him, too. Maybe he wasn't as stupid and unimaginative as I had thought.

"And part of me thinks that's what your mother really likes about me. I may be boring, but I have one or two of the old-fashioned virtues that often go along with that. I'm steady and reliable and predictable, too. Maybe she needs that. Sometimes I honestly believe that is a side of me she likes to have near her. I know your sister does."

He turned and smiled.

"And I think I rather hoped that, one day, you might too."

There's no way to answer a remark like that. Oh, you can drift upstairs after a bit, and think about it all you like; but there's no answer you can really give except to shrug in an embarrassed way and smile back, and I did both those. But, later, lying in bed waiting for Mum, I wondered if I hadn't been a bit unfair on poor old Gerald Faulkner, deciding so early on that he was the worst thing to have happened to our household since Dad packed his boxes and went off to Inverness. After all, if you thought about it, it wasn't really Gerald's fault that Mum seemed so much brighter and merrier when she had his company as well, and not just ours. Or that she went out to the cinema so often right after she first met him. She could have said no, and stayed home. (I got a bit of a guilt pang when I remembered she'd tried that and I'd gotten even more bad-tempered!) No. I'd not been all that fair.

And it had been a bit mean, too, to blame poor Goggle-eyes just because he liked to see Mum in her fanciest clothes, and thought she had nice legs. Simon thought Mum had nice legs. So did Dad, when he bothered to say so. What was so wrong, for heaven's sake, with simply liking someone's legs?

I was still lying there in the dark, wondering why on earth I'd gone so berserk that first evening, when Mum came home.

I don't know why I didn't throw back the covers and rush downstairs to greet her at once. Perhaps, if I had, the ghastly, ghastly quarrel between Mum and Goggle-eyes would never have had the time to happen. So why did I stay upstairs, lurking so quietly under the blankets pretending I was fast asleep? Was it really only because I was exhausted and the bed was so toasty warm? Or was it because, right from the moment Mum slammed through the front door, shaking the walls and shouting, "I'm home, folks!" so triumphantly, I could tell there was trouble brewing.

"Rosalind! Please! The girls are fast asleep. Don't make so much noise!"

I can imagine the look that came over Mum's face at this sort of greeting.

"Is this the welcome for the conquering heroine?"

When he answered his voice was muffled, but I could still hear.

"There's nothing heroic about waking two exhausted children."

Mum sounded even more reproachful now.

"You might have let them stay up!"

"Kept them up, you mean? Just to cheer you in? That's a bit self-indulgent, isn't it, when they've got school in the morning?"

I expect she was all cold and cross after hours of hanging around in the police station, and then the long ride home.

"They would have been a lot more welcoming than you!"

"Naturally. They've been a lot better indoctrinated than I have into believing that what you're doing is important."

What were those thuds? Were they just her muddy boots hitting the floor, one after another?

"It *is* important."

"Some people might say that getting yourself arrested on the spur of the moment is not so much important as irresponsible!"

Now that was *definitely* the coat closet door being slammed shut. I know what she's like when she's getting really annoyed. I bet she even swung around and put her hands on her hips before starting in on him properly.

"Now listen, Gerald. It's good of you to bring the girls home and stay with them. I'm very grateful. But I'm not prepared to stand here and listen to abuse, and I don't take kindly to being called irresponsible by you. I am not irresponsible!" Her voice was rising now, louder and louder. She was working herself up. "I think very hard before I take either of my children on anything like this. I don't take them anywhere the army is — I've seen how mean and rough and badly disciplined those boys can be! I don't take them anywhere there's horses, or barbed wire. I don't take them anywhere at night, or anywhere things might get out of hand. So don't you dare call me irresponsible!"

She was shouting at him now. Shouting at him good and hard. I wasn't at all surprised to see Jude float like a wraith through the dimly lit shape of my open bedroom doorway, and feel her climbing in my bed at my side.

"She'll stop in a minute," I whispered. "She's just very cold and tired and hungry, and he said the wrong thing."

She didn't stop. She was so cold and tired and hungry she let him have it like a meat-ax between the eyes. I'm amazed that the neighbors didn't start pounding on the walls — or perhaps they preferred listening? They could have listened while she yelled at him that she was sick to death of having to go out and make such efforts. And she was angry — yes, *angry* — more angry than he could imagine or she could say! Angry enough to leave home and band with thousands and thousands of others to keep a vigil around the miles of wire fences that hid these fiendish, stupid, cripplingly expensive weapons from all the

140

people who were paying for them, and in whose name the lovely green planet we were living on might soon be changed into a smoking ball of rubble.

"You say it's kept the peace!" she yelled. "Peace? Call this *peace?* Don't be so stupid, Gerald! Don't be so blind! This isn't *peace.* Peace is security. Peace is living in *confidence.* This — this is like being six miles high in a tinny airplane thinking you feel quite safe, then, the moment a little bit of turbulence hits you, realizing you are actually *terrified,* and would sell your soul to have both feet firmly fixed on good brown earth!"

"You!" she shrieked. "People like you are the dangerous ones now! People like you who are so dense, so stubborn, so gullible! Go on! Ignore the billions of pounds wasted each year on these terrible weapons. Go on! Ignore the risks the power stations might explode, or start leaking worse than they do already. Carry on, Gerald! Believe the government 'experts,' though you know well enough they've lied to you again and again! And don't forget to ignore the generations of children forced to grow up fearing they'll blow up! Go on, Gerald! Go home and put your head in a paper bag! Keep goggling away at your important share prices and your important interest rates! Don't act irresponsibly, for heaven's sake! Don't worry about our frail little green planet!"

I was hugging Jude tight now, to stop her trembling.

"He won't yell back at her," I whispered. "He won't, I promise. He won't stay and fight. He won't lose his temper and he won't hit her. He's steady and reliable and predictable. You can depend on Gerald. He will just go."

That's what he did. We didn't hear a word — only the door as he pulled it closed behind him, and then, through the bedroom window, his footsteps ringing down our front walk.

You can depend on Gerald. He just went.

8
xxx

Ⅰɴ the gloom of the closet it was hard
to see Helen's face clearly, but it was pretty obvious
the idea of Goggle-eyes striding out hopelessly into
the storm was not her idea of a fairy-tale ending.

"Poor Kitty! How awful! You must have been horribly upset!"

I told you back at the start that Helen is a softie.
I couldn't help teasing her a little bit.

"Horribly upset?" I repeated. "Is that how you'd
feel if your mother and the gray-haired Whatsisname
break up?"

She shook her head.

"It's not the same," she told me firmly. "Goggle-
eyes sounds nice really, underneath, once you've got
used to him a bit. Toad-shoes is different."

(So that was his name. I'd found out at last. Toad-
shoes.)

Helen leaned forward confidentially to explain.

"You see," she said. "Toad-shoes is *awful*. I'll tell you what he's like. He's — "

A violent clattering on the door interrupted her. The knob rattled and the panels shook. Stray meteorites colliding with Lost Property Capsule? No, Liz. Her voice came through the panels loud and clear.

"Hey, you guys! Have you any idea how long you've been in there? Loopy is definitely panicking. She says you must be running short of air. She's sent me down with a message."

"What message?" I yelled back.

Long pause. Liz isn't all that bright. She has to run a huge computer search in order to locate a four-word newsflash. Finally, among some rusty, slow-functioning components of gray matter, she found it.

"Be out by lunch!"

Lunch? Helen stared at me, and clapped her hand over her mouth in horror.

Lunch? Yes, come to think of it, I was feeling hungry. And peering at the face of my watch, I saw that, sure enough, it was already after twelve.

"Helen, we've been in here nearly *three hours*."

Behind her hand, Helen just giggled. Meanwhile, Liz the Galactic Intercom was yelling through the door:

"You've missed a huge lecture about making a mess in the art room. And a surprise chemistry test. And putting chairs out for the senior recital. And angles associated with parallel lines."

"Good," I yelled. "What are we missing now?"

"Now?" Liz ran through one of her laborious brain printouts. "Now you are missing French — revision of irregular past participles."

"You'd better hop along, Liz," I suggested. "You of all people surely don't want to miss that!"

After the couple of seconds it took her to process this, Liz started beating on the door panels again.

"Helen?" she shouted. "Helen? Are you still in there?"

I ask you! What a stupid question!

Helen's so sweet and patient. "Yes," she called back. "I'm still in here, Liz. Honestly."

Liz tapped again. You'd think we were two miners trapped hundreds of feet underground behind tons of fallen rock-face. You wouldn't for a moment think that all Liz had to do was stop her demented rattling of the door knob for one single second, and *pull* it, for all to be revealed.

I was just gathering breath to bellow, "Push off, Liz!" when Helen called out:

"Tell you what! Save me a seat at lunch, and we'll sit together. I shall be out in a few minutes."

There's tact for you. And it does work. Liz, when she answered, sounded really cheerful.

"Fine!" she called. "See you at lunchtime, Helen."

The mad rattling of the doorknob stopped at last. Suddenly it seemed very quiet in the cupboard.

"Go on," Helen said (rather imperiously for her, I thought). "Quick. Get on with the story. What happened when Gerald turned up on the doorstep with armfuls of flowers? Did your mother forgive him, or did the poor old sausage get the Big Freeze?"

Inasmuch as it's possible to stare at someone through dimly lit murk, I stared at Helen Johnston. So Goggle-eyes had been transmuted into "Poor Old Sausage" now, had he? Honestly! If her sweet nature could, in the space of a morning, turn Gerald Faulkner into an object of tender sympathy, it probably wouldn't be more than a couple of weeks before Toad-shoes, creeping warily through the back door, found Helen's arms wrapped around him in cheerful welcome. My mission, clearly, was all but accomplished. It had been easier than I thought.

Well. No point in holding back close to the goal line. So I finished the story.

➔ BIG FREEZE? Big Freeze? I tell you, what Gerald Faulkner would have met if he'd walked up our path was not so much the Big Freeze as the Original Permafrost. Good thing he never risked it. There would have been icicles hanging from his silvery locks before he so much as stepped on our doormat (which might still *say* WELCOME in carefully woven and dyed two-tone sisal, but which definitely wouldn't have *meant* it). I don't think I've ever seen an expression as vinegary as the one on Mum's face when she drew those miserable shriveled chops and poor little blackened peas out from their overnight charring in the oven.

"Take my advice, Kits," she said to me a shade incomprehensibly, but with unmistakable venom. "Never confuse a man's concern for your physical welfare with his support for any of the rest of you!"

"No, Mum," I said. (Best not to argue, I've always found, when you can see the bags under their eyes.) "Didn't you sleep?"

"Sleep?" she snapped, pushing her tangled hair back from her pale, drawn face. "Of course I slept. Why shouldn't I sleep, for heaven's sake? Naturally I slept like a log, all night. What on earth makes you think I couldn't sleep?"

And that was that!

What a *nerve!* I was so angry that I banged the door at her when I went off to school. Parents really push their luck. If they decide it's inconvenient for you to know things or have strong feelings about them, then you don't know them and you don't have feelings — simple as that! When she's in love with Goggle-eyes, she doesn't even notice that I hate his guts, he makes my flesh creep, and I wish him dead. Then, over weeks and weeks, it becomes obvious to me that, if I don't like him, I am going to have to lump him. And since I actually happen to *live* here, since this is my *home,* if you've noticed, I'd rather not lump it. It makes me miserable. So I make this jumbo-sized effort to come to terms with Gerald Faulkner, talk to him, see his good points, admit that he's really important to Jude, and that he tries hard.

And then — poof! Just because he has one major fight with my mother one night, Gerald is banished for good. And, once again, Mum simply goes and blinds herself to everyone else's feelings. That can't be Jude, you know, sitting so glumly on the sofa with her thumb in her mouth and Floss curled in her lap. Oh, no. That woeful little person can't be Jude because, if it were, that might mean Jude's actually sitting there missing somebody she actually cares for, somebody precious to her. And Mum's decided that person no longer exists.

"Look, Mum!" Jude charges into the kitchen every other morning. "Gerald's sent me another postcard!"

"Gerald?" (You know the tone of voice: Gerald? Gerald who? Do I know someone called Gerald?) Not the response to encourage someone as shy as Jude to talk a little about how she's missing him.

It makes me very angry. It's very dishonest. After all, it's not as if Gerald were just Mum's, to keep or drop as she chooses. Jude had become close to him too, for better or worse. They spent a lot of time together. He helped her with her homework. She depended on him. You could say he was even getting to be a little bit like another father. I tell you, the day I wandered in the sitting room and caught Jude trying to read the stock-market report to herself, moving her lips and using her finger to try to keep her place on the enormous page, I nearly burst into tears, honestly I did.

And I missed him too, to be perfectly honest. At first I only missed all the little things that you'd expect: the bright fizzy drinks; the boxes of chocolates; get-

148

ting the radiator in my room fixed as soon as it went on the blink — that kind of thing. But then, as weeks went by, I started missing all sorts of other things, like Mum sometimes being in those really good moods that came from having someone standing around admiring her for hours on end. Oh, she did invite poor old Standby Simon around quite a few times (especially the week Jude started on multiplication of decimals!). But it wasn't the same. How could it be? Simon is really nice, but he isn't Gerald.

And I know Mum missed Gerald too. I could tell. Sometimes I caught her staring at the telephone. One day I even watched her sitting beside it for half an hour, wondering whether to pick it up and dial. But she never cracked. Even that Saturday morning when I told her I was going to the library, and I knew from the way her voice went all drab and flat as she answered that, like me, she was remembering the time she chased me around the kitchen table, laughing and trying to snatch my library card, and Gerald caught her in his arms.

I'll tell you what else I missed — his little acid-drop remarks. Like when we walked past a man shouting "Equal pay for all!" and Gerald whispered to me: "Mark my words, there speaks a poor man." And when it was my turn to take the gerbils at the end of the term, and by the time I finally staggered into the house with the cage, it turned out the two of them had chewed up my report card, every last word. Mum's face went dark. I think she thought I'd fed the stiff brown envelope through the bars deliberately. I think she was just on the verge of ripping my ears off when Gerald somehow got in first, sarcastically suggesting we try to sell the cage as a cheap, efficient, and ecologically sound shredding machine. Mum fell over laughing, and I was saved.

I wasn't the only person he rescued, either. I'd not forgotten that awful Sunday night Jude panicked utterly because she suddenly remembered she was supposed to learn a whole poem about "Winter" for first thing Monday morning. The library was closed. Jude tore around the house half frantic, close to tears, begging us to stop whatever we were doing and just *think, please! Somebody* must remember a poem about winter — a really short one she could learn in time.

So good old Gerald sighed and laid down his paper, and sat on the sofa, pondering. And then suddenly the light of memory flashed in his eye, and, standing up, he grasped the lapels of his jacket like a town councilor in a TV serial, and solemnly declaimed the shortest winter poem he could dredge from his cultured past:

> *Ladies and Gentlemen,*
> *Take my advice,*
> *Pull down your knickers,*
> *And slide on the ice.*

Jude thought it was the funniest poem she'd ever heard. She laughed so hard she stopped her terrible worrying altogether, and managed to learn the whole of "When Icicles Hang by the Wall" before morning. (It turned out good old Gerald knew that, too.)

It wasn't often Gerald could surprise you. But I was really surprised to find out how much I ended up missing having him around. So was Mrs. Lupey. When I handed in my sonnet "Gerald — A Lament," she only raised her eyebrows a little. But when she gave me back my essay "The Person I Miss Most," she said she found it very moving indeed, and the sincerity of my feelings showed even through the rather tasteless jokes with which it was most unfortunately studded.

Give Gerald his due, he did his best to keep in touch with us without annoying Mum. The postcards he sent Jude came regularly; but each had some special picture or joke on the front that let him off the hook, as if he were saying: "I happened to notice this card, and I couldn't resist it." (One was a cat that looked exactly like our Floss, for example. Jude used it to make Floss a "real" passport. And another was a blackboard covered all over in terrifying mathematical symbols. Poor Jude went pale.) And, on the back, though he wrote something different every time, he always somehow managed to imply that his fondness for Jude remained unchanged, while mere force of circumstance kept him regrettably stuck on his side of town.

And I got something from him, too, after a couple of weeks. It was a copy of a reply from the commander of the submarine base, and pretty weaseling and apologetic it was too (though there was no mention of chipping in for the drycleaning of the suit). Mum said he only bothered to reply at all because Gerald made a point of sending copies of his complaint both to his Member of Parliament and to the First Sea Lord of the Admiralty. But that was just sour grapes. After all, if enough people took the time, like Gerald, to complain loudly and bitterly all around whenever they were splattered with mud by the police or the armed forces, some people's desks would soon be armpit-high in disgruntled taxpayers' letters, and in the end the men in charge would probably find it less trouble to order their underlings to be more civil.

Mum's mouth set like a trap when I said this, but she was in a bad mood anyhow. Mind you, she had an excuse. Each day her court case crept a little nearer, and she was getting nervous. You see, she didn't know whether to plead guilty or not. Pleading not guilty was a lot more bother, but it's the only way to get to say your piece. And, apprehensive as she was, Mum felt she ought to stand up in Sheriff's Court and defend her actions. So day after day around the house, we'd come across her delivering impassioned speeches to herself like a mad bag-lady, insisting these weapons were "a potential crime against humanity as wrong as the gas chambers of Auschwitz," or that "the citizen of a free country has both a right and a duty to act by his or her own conscience," or "silence implies consent, so I won't stay silent." She should have been a lawyer, honestly. She was very convincing. You'd sneak up on her in the kitchen, and she'd be standing with her arms in the sink, telling the geranium on the window sill: "No! It can *never* be morally right to use these ghastly weapons at any time, whether first, or as unthinkable retaliation after we ourselves are doomed!" Or, making the bed, she'd ask the pillows as she plumped them up: "Tell me — a child dies of hunger every few seconds while we spend a million a day on nuclear weapons. Do you think that's *right?* Is that what you *want?*"

After a couple of weeks of this, I reckoned our house plants and our pillows must, like those sheep around the submarine base, know more about nuclear issues than the average Scottish voter. But in the end all these imaginative rehearsals of her few glorious moments in court had quite the opposite effect. By the big morning, she was for chickening out.

"Chickening out?"

"That's right." She slammed my breakfast down in front of me as if I'd been arguing, not just asking. "I'm going to go there, plead guilty, pay the fine, and come straight home. I've done my bit."

"Fair enough." (She'd been so irritable stamping through the house making political speeches that part of me was relieved. And it would be wonderful to come home from school and find Mum her old self again, interested in my day at school, not too distracted to help Jude with her homework, happy to sit and watch the news without muttering darkly whenever some malefactor's face flashed on the screen: "That's who the police should be watching, you know — not upright citizens like me!").

I really enjoyed that day. It went so fast. Between lessons I kept thinking about Mum, imagining her case going through court like clockwork, thinking how glad she'd be that the whole business was over at last, how good it would be to charge through the front door yelling, "Mum! Mum! Are you back?" and see her poking her head around the kitchen door, grinning her head off.

I couldn't wait to get home. I even jumped off the bus at the stop by the rotary and ran across the park, because it's quicker. I pelted up the walk and flung myself against the front door, tugging at the catch.

It was still locked. I was a bit surprised. It didn't matter, since I could let myself in with my own key; but all the same it was unsettling. And though I still hoped that for some reason she'd gone all the way around the house and let herself in at the back door, really I knew, however loudly I called through the echoing hall and up the stairs, she wasn't going to be there to answer.

It seemed a very long wait. It was lonely, too. Jude wasn't coming home — she'd been sent to a friend's house, just in case — and I couldn't settle. I spread my homework books across the table, and stealing handful after handful of currants from the dried-fruit jar, I watched the clock.

Four-thirty. Five. No sign of her. No phone call.

At five-fifteen I cracked, and rang Gerald's office. The secretary would have let me speak to him, I know. But Gerald wasn't there.

"Hasn't been in all day," he said cheerfully.

"Do you know where he is?"

"I've no idea." And then he added: "All I can tell you is that Mr. Faulkner said it was something special, and he was not sure when he would be back."

I put the phone down slowly. Something special . . . In the mirror, when I looked up, I saw I was grinning. I knew where Gerald was. Gerald — so steady and reliable and, yes, predictable. Not at all the sort of person to stop caring for someone just because she is in a mega-huff about some serious issue they disagree on, and extra jumpy waiting to go to court. No. Gerald's the sort of person who can wait.

I sat down in front of my books, and did my homework without so much as another sideways glance at the clock. I didn't have to worry about Mum any longer. Even if she was still hopping mad at him (and, knowing her, she probably was) it didn't matter. He would still be there, sitting at the back of the court, seeing that everything went as it should — making sure no one told lies about what she did, or bullied her; lending her money to pay her fine if she'd forgotten her checkbook; making sure she got home safe . . .

She didn't get home till quarter to seven. Her entrance was as immodest as usual.

"Ta-*ra!* Enter the heroine! Crack open the champagne!"

I pushed my books away, and ran to hug her.

"Are you all right?"

"All right?" She swirled around, skirts flying. "Am I all right? I'm better than all right. I am *magnificent!*"

"What happened? Why are you so excited?"

(I wondered suddenly if Goggle-eyes had captured her outside the court, shoved a ring on her finger, and made her agree to marry him.)

"What happened? I'll tell you what happened. I was *wonderful.*"

"Were you acquitted?"

"Acquitted?" She looked blank for a moment. "No, I don't think I was acquitted. I think I was discharged."

"What's the difference?"

She reached out for my hands, and spun me around. "Oh, how should I know, Kitty? I'm not a lawyer." Then, dropping my hands, she kept on spinning around by herself. "But I should be. I made the best speech in the world!"

"How come?" I interrupted her. "How come you got to make a speech at all? I thought you told me you were going to plead guilty."

She blushed. (That's not like her.)

"I was. But then I got a bit confused, and pleaded the wrong way."

"That's not like you."

"I told you, I got confused."

"Why?" I asked suddenly. She's not the only one

who'd make a good lawyer. I myself have a pretty cunning line in subtle prosecution questions. "Why did you get confused? Was there anyone sitting in court you were surprised to see?"

She stopped her spinning and peered at me suspiciously.

"You *knew*," she accused me. "You knew he'd be there! You could have warned me, Kitty. He practically startled me out of my wits. You've no idea what a shock it was to see him sitting there between the Quakers and Flowery Headscarf's supporters from St. Thomas and St. James, glowering at me."

"At least he turned up."

She grinned.

"Oh, yes," she said. "He turned up. And since he startled me into pleading not guilty, he got to hear my historic statement."

She would have started off the swirling and spinning again, but I stopped her.

"Right," I said. "He had to sit there and listen to you. So now it's your turn. Give him a call."

Mum stared.

"Give him a call? Why?"

I stared her out.

"Because," I said. "I miss him. I'd like to see him. And so would Jude. You saw him today, but we didn't, so now it's our turn. You call him up and ask him over here."

For a moment I thought she would argue. But she opened her mouth and then closed it again. It was clear she was thinking. And obviously one day had made a big difference in how she felt about things. Yesterday she was all wound up about the court case. Now the worry was over, and nothing could spoil her mood. She even felt good about Gerald. She was pleased that he'd taken the trouble to turn up and support her. She was pleased he still cared. And I think she was even pleased that we missed him and, especially, that I — the one who used to be his worst enemy in our house — would even come right out and say so.

Mrs. Lupey says living successfully in a family is largely a matter of timing. I think I must have picked exactly the right moment.

"All right," she said. "I'll call him. I don't mind. We'll have him over tonight if he's free."

"He's free," I told her. "He's been free for weeks."

Of course he was free. I didn't have to eavesdrop on Mum's end of the call for more than a few seconds before it was quite clear he'd be around at our house in almost no time at all. Then Mum remembered suddenly which way he comes. "Oh, please, Gerald. On your way, would you pick Jude up from Hetty's?"

I don't know what he answered. But I can guess what he felt. I know how Jude felt, anyway, because Hetty's dad told us later Jude threw herself into Gerald's arms with such force he was astonished Gerald wasn't more seriously winded than he was.

They both looked fine by the time they arrived home. I let them in, since Mum was still upstairs. He strode through the door and hugged me tightly. His pockets were absolutely bulging with lemons.

"You'll ruin your suit," I warned him. "It'll go baggy."

"I don't care!"

He swung me around. (It seemed to be National Make-Kitty-Dizzy Day.)

"Your mother was *wonderful* in court," he told me. "She was *magnificent*. She made the best speech in the world!"

I grinned.

"I know," I said. "She already told me."

"Glad to know her total lack of modesty remains undimmed," he remarked (quite charitably considering the way he'd been treated, I thought), and set to work — steadily, reliably, and predictably — with knife and chopping board, ice cubes and lemons.

⚓ AND THAT'S how we go on. He's around a lot. I can't say he's altered any of his views. He still thinks I ought to keep my room clean and tidy, and open my blinds first thing in the morning, and not eat between meals. He still goes around the house complaining: "These lights are on again! I've just been around and switched them all off. Now they're all on again!" He hasn't changed.

Mum has, though. He's got her firmly on his side now. She's on my back every Saturday morning, thrusting the duster into my hand, parking the vacuum cleaner outside my door. "Give it to Jude after you've finished," she tells me. "She has to clean hers, too." (At least everything's fair now.) Mum's back to being as tough with us as she used to be before Dad left. I think Gerald gives her the moral support that she needs to keep battling. She's even stopped paying me for the potatoes.

He's still got the old sharp tongue. You can't organize a street collection or a demonstration without getting a barrage from Gerald about how you ought to be doing it differently, or more efficiently, or somewhere else. But he's been very helpful. His little printing firm runs off all our fliers and information sheets now, and I can't believe it's really all quite as cheap as he tells me. But he never comes along on demonstrations anymore. He just sits at home with his feet up, reading the paper. We don't mind. After all, he was only an embarrassment. And when we come home now, crabby and exhausted, we never have to stop off at McDonald's. He always has something delicious waiting.

I don't know how long things will last between him and Mum. You'd think it would be difficult to spend so much time with someone who thinks so differently about the world. But there have been no great explosions between them since that day when she went to court. Mum claims that's because, secretly, though Gerald won't admit it, he was completely won around by her eloquence to our point of view. Gerald says that's nonsense. He says all that happened that day was that he finally understood what it all meant to her. He said she stood there, leaning on the rail, telling the whole court about the paint peeling off the walls in her hospital, and babies brought in gray-faced from coughing in damp rooms, and crippled children staring bleakly out of rain-splattered windows because their wheelchair batteries have run down and there's no one to change them. And how the sheer waste of it breaks her heart. So many people struggling night and day to care for those they love against tremendous odds, while little cliques of self-important rulers and blinkered soldiers play senseless and expensive war games.

"And it's *our* planet," said Mum. "Ours more than theirs. There's more of us. And when we go to all the trouble and strain of raising our children properly, we want to know that there's a future. If we take time preparing proper meals and making our children practice their musical instruments, we want to know the chances are that they'll grow up and there will always be music.

"That's why I cut the wire," Mum said. "Because all day I work with people who need help. And I know more money is spent on these shiny new missiles than is ever spent on the people these missiles are supposed to be defending. And if things don't change, more and more people are going to come to believe the way they're living isn't worth protecting."

Gerald says he hasn't changed his own mind at all.

But now he understands better why Mum acts as she does. Next time, he says with a sly grin, he'll support her more strongly, and look after both of us so she can go to jail. (She always smiles back so sweetly when he says this, but, if I know Mum, it won't be so long before poor Gerald finds he's been taken up on his very kind offer, and she's been sent to jail for a month!)

I wouldn't mind. I get along with Gerald really well now. Dad sometimes asks, when he phones up from Inverness:

"No sign of wedding bells yet?"

And I say:

"No. Not yet."

But, thinking about it a couple of nights ago, I realized things have changed more than I ever could have imagined since the day when he first came to our house. I still think the way he thinks is crazy, of course. Nuclear weapons cost the earth and they could cost us the earth. But I can live with him. He still thinks there are reds under the beds, but even Gerald's slowly coming round to the view that better some are red than all are dead.

Mum says not to worry. Like everyone else with any sense at all, he'll have to come around in the end. She even got him out last week, marching in support of her nurses. (Trust Gerald! He turned up at the hospital carrying a banner that said RECTIFY THE ANOMALY. Mum nearly died!)

He still won't join the antinuclear movement, though. I don't mind any more. I just feel so sorry for him that he's too blind to see what I see, too numb to feel what I feel. Sometimes when I go leaping and hopping down the street, and the air's crisp and sharp, and the leaves crackle under my feet, and the sun slides out from behind clouds like shining silver, I think that Gerald can't ever have felt this happy, not even when he was young. For, if he had, he'd surely make more of an effort now to help us save the lovely little green planet we're living on, so others can take their turn for ever and ever.

And sometimes, when he's lolling about on the sofa on Sunday mornings, testing Jude on her knowledge of the stockmarket, I don't even bother thinking that. I just find him soothing and amiable and steady — easy to have around. I'm used to him, I suppose. He's part of the furniture. I honestly believe, if he and Mum got married, I wouldn't mind.

➤ "YOU wouldn't *mind?*"
"No. I don't think so."
"Not at *all?*"
"Not really, no."
"Hmmm."
She wrinkled her nose suspiciously, but she didn't argue. She just sat tight for a few moments, thinking. I didn't disturb her.
Then:

"Of course, Toad-shoes is different. He's not like Goggle-eyes at all. He's awful. I'll tell you what he's like. He's —"

A frightful banging on the door interrupted her. I thought for a moment this was Liz again, back to screech another public-service announcement through the lost-property closet door. But this particular visitor was no ineffectual knob-rattling slouch. With one sharp tug, the door flew open. Helen and I were blinded by the light.

Mission Control.

I don't think, for all her great insight, Mrs. Lupey is any more cut out to be a Samaritan than I am. Considering the last time she set eyes on Helen Johnston she was a gibbering, blubbering wreck, I thought the tone of voice was somewhat waspish:

"Are you two *ever* planning to come out?"

I stumbled to my feet. Oh, agony! Pins and needles! While I was doubled over with pain, grinding my foot against the floor, Mrs. Lupey put poor old Helen through the third degree.

"Feeling better, dear?"

"Yes, thank you, Mrs. Lupey. I'm lots better. I think I'm fine now, honestly."

"You don't want to go home?"

"No, really. I'm all right. I feel much better."

"You've been in this closet for an awfully long time."

"Kitty's been telling me a story."

164

"Oh, yes?" She turned toward me, and I think she winked. "I'll say one thing for Kitty. She spins a good yarn."

Helen was busy now, brushing the bits of fluff off the sleeves of her sweater. She answered perfectly cheerfully:

"I can't *believe* Kitty and I have been in here all morning!"

"Oh, well," said Mrs. Lupey, standing back to let her out. "That is the power of the storyteller for you."

(It's one of Loopy's Great Theories. She's always going on about it. Living your life is a long and doggy business, says Mrs. Lupey. And stories and books help. Some help you with the living itself. Some help you just take a break. The best do both at the same time.)

She may be right. One way or the other, I'd certainly cheered up Helen Johnston. She strode right out of that closet smiling, and, patting me warmly on the hand for thanks, ran off upstairs to have lunch with Liz without so much as a backward look.

Mrs. Lupey took hold of my shoulders, and turned me to face her.

"Well done," she said. "I knew that I could count on you. You've done a good job, Number Twenty-two."

Fortunately she was as hungry as I was. She didn't hang around to find out any details about what was bothering Helen Johnston. She took straight off.

Good thing, too. I'd have been stumped to tell her anything except the villain's name: Toad-shoes. And I'm still standing by, waiting to hear the full story. Helen's so busy and cheerful again these days, she won't take the time off to fill me in with all the grisly details.

I'll just have to keep waiting. And so will you.